Once Upon a
WICKED
EVE

Dark Tales and Dreadful Wonders

Rick Jurewicz

**DIRE HAND
PUBLISHING**

PO Box 2144, Indian River, Michigan 49749

Copyright © 2019 Rick Jurewicz
Cover Design Copyright © 2019 Rick Jurewicz
Illustrations Copyright © 2019 Rick Jurewicz

Cover design and layout by John Dropchuk
Interior illustrations by Madison Smith

All rights reserved. This book or any portion thereof
may not be reproduced or used in any manner whatsoever
without the express written permission of the publisher
except for the use of brief quotations in a book review.

These stories are works of fiction. Names, characters, businesses, places,
events and incidents are either the products of the author's imagination or
used in a fictitious manner. Any resemblance to actual persons, living or
dead, or actual events is purely coincidental.

ISBN: 0578584298
ISBN-13: 978-0578584294

For all who dare to
dream dark dreams,
play in the shadows
and peek at the monster
hiding beneath their
beds...these tales
are for you.

Contents

Introduction	viii
To Catch a Crow	3
The Pale-Faced Man	23
They Say it Happened	39
The Bond	63
Dark Little Corner – A Poem	103
Justice	105
Ol' Halloween – A Poem	127
The Pumpkin Patch of Ernie Manville	129
One Dark Soul – A Poem	151
Matchmaker	153
The Crossroads Gambit	213
I am a Butterfly	235

Rick Jurewicz

INTRODUCTION

Welcome to the Edge. The imperceptible line that separates everything one could ever want and desire from their deepest and darkest fears...those fears that dwell in the lost and forgotten caverns of the human heart and soul.

Wander the narrow and rocky path that crosses over, around and through this frightening and fascinating twilight realm of imagination, where your nightmares crawl, by tooth and by claw, into the reality you thought was the safe haven around you. A world where even the things for which you dream and desire can lead you down a road of madness that can even make your nightmares seem like a place of sanctuary from the cold grip of reality...

Meet a curmudgeon of a man with an appetite for a delicacy that nature never intended for consumption, and the cost that is far greater than any reward he could have ever imagined...

Four boys stalk the night on All Hallows Eve on what might be their last trick-or-treating year together, as they themselves are stalked by both a mysterious figure and a dark twist of fate...

Horror loving teenage friends plan a last blast summer adventure before the coming school year by way of exploring a popular local urban legend site, but find diving too far into the rabbit hole can have devastating consequences...

Twin brothers with an unbreakable bond are touched by a tragedy that put that bond to the test across the boundaries of life and death while seeking the answers to a mystery shrouded in murder, betrayal and devastating loss...

Privilege and wealth may protect a young and vile man from the clutches of the law, but the shadow cast by his deeds stirs a darkness that he may not be able to escape, born from a heart filled with both love and a desire for justice by any means necessary...

Three teens looking to make some quick cash hatch a scheme that puts them in a pumpkin patch on Halloween night. When things take an unfortunate and tragic turn, an unworldly force deep within the vine-twisted soils seeks retribution for the wrongs wrought upon those very grounds...

A snarky yet poignant goth girl and a desperately lovesick young woman find a unique connection in their shared struggle with obsession, infatuation, love, friendship, relationships, self discovery, personal awakenings...and a cursed coffee shop table that can bring you your hearts deepest desire. But getting what one thinks they want may be more than one can bear...

A young man with big dreams and aspirations follows an old legend to a crossroads at midnight, looking to make a deal. But he is a man with a plan, and has every intention to beat the deal at all costs. Will saving his soul be enough to beat this "devil"?

...and, a story about a butterfly? Things aren't always as they seem...

Venture along with these souls, both lost and found, watching over your own shoulder as you carry on down this dark and winding road,
Once Upon a Wicked Eve...

Rick Jurewicz

Rick Jurewicz

ONCE UPON A
WICKED
EVE

Dark Tales and Dreadful Wonders

Rick Jurewicz

To CATCH a CROW

Old Mr. Shumple lived on the outskirts of a small town in an old and weather-worn decrepit three-room shack that should have been condemned as dangerous and unlivable years ago. But given the oddity and lore surrounding the "crazy-old-coot", for the most part, he was left alone to his own devices.

Once a week, he would make the six-mile trek into town to gather his essentials, as minimal as they might have been, and what a sight he was to behold as passers-by would note when he made his way down the last two miles of the main highway on his way to the market. He was a tall man, about six-foot-six, with a long and unkempt beard, mostly gray, but considerably yellowed throughout, often with flecks of whatever his most recent meal may have been trapped in its entanglements. Whether it be January or July, Mr. Shumple wore a dirty green knit hat upon his head, and cotton gloves with the fingers cut off. His trousers were dark and tattered, boots worn but whole, and an old beaten Carhartt jacket that extended below his waist covering a blue, button down dress shirt that had as well seen better days. This was all anyone ever saw the old man wear.

For those that did not know better, who would try and offer certain charities to the old man, they would find themselves scoffed and grunted at, and Mr. Shumple would rudely turn them away. It was not because he was a proud man. No, Mr. Shumple had great disdain for *everyone*. He wanted nothing to do with the outside world, and dreaded every minute of the weekly journey to town for things that he needed, eventually to the point where the list of items he went after grew shorter and shorter.

First, certain toiletries were omitted from his needs list; he then cut out any sorts of treats he might offer himself, such as snack cakes and hard candies, just to lessen the time he had to spend around other people in the grocery store. But it was the absence of toiletries and personal hygiene products that caused those he would shop around to equally want him to hasten his shopping venture. This suited him fine. Over time, his senses had weakened, and the foulness that had overtaken his essence did not bother him in the least. He was aware of it, as he was aware of his foul temperament to the outside world, but he did not care about it anymore than he cared what others had thought of it.

No one knew why Mr. Shumple was the way that he was. He was a mystery, and as such provoked much speculation, especially in the minds of small town folk. Many thought that he was mad, suffering from some form of psychosis or other derangement. Others thought that perhaps he was burdened by both madness and genius, like one of those people who shunned modern technological society or held a grudge against the government. Whatever it was, those who met the cold gaze of his eyes when they looked upon his grizzled face knew enough to stay away, and it even got to the point in the local market where the checkout girls knew not to even try and exchange simple pleasantries as they would with any other customer who came through their checkout line. Whenever there was a new cashier working the line, and when the management saw him heading for the front, the new worker would be replaced with another more experienced one until the transaction was through, and Mr. Shumple had left the store.

    Everything went mostly smooth, although there had been occasions where something didn't scan correctly at the cash register, and Mr. Shumple would go into a fit about taxes, the government, and everyone trying to cheat him and steal his money. He always paid with cash, which of course led to speculation that he was secretly wealthy and had money hidden away in the walls of his home or buried in a box somewhere in the woods. But anyone who had kicked around the idea of going and snooping for themselves to see if the rumors might be true would drive out past the cruddy blue and gray shack that had paint peeling in every direction, and they would decide not to ever bother with the thought any further. There were the others who would not even get that far, passing the old man as he went through the town, and they would catch a glimpse of his cold, pale blue eyes and decide that whatever horrors they might face in a lonely encounter with this man were not worth the risk of something as remote as a hidden fortune. And so, Mr. Shumple would get his wish. He was left alone.

    It was one of those return trips from town on an unbearably hot and humid day in late August that Mr. Shumple had once more been reminded of the disgust he held for his fellow man. Although most people did not try and push the man's buttons, that much could not always be said for the rowdy and rambunctious local youths. Mr. Shumple was within a mile from his home, pulling behind him a small makeshift cart that he himself had built with old wooden crates and bicycle wheels, and two old shovel handles that extended from the cart causing it to resemble a small rickshaw. He paid no attention to the sound of a vehicle coming up fast behind him. When the small pickup truck was finally upon him, it slowed down just as it passed. The brake lights came on, and the truck slid in the dusty gravel to a stop. Three teenage boys popped up from the bed of the truck and started to throw water balloons at Mr. Shumple, but the balloons had also been loaded with dish soap as well, covering Mr. Shumple in slippery suds and water.

"Take a bath you smelly old man," yelled one of the boys as the others whooped and hollered and laughed. The driver of the truck hit the gas, spinning the tires wildly, throwing rocks and dust at Mr. Shumple, who in turned yelled profanities and raised his fist into the air, waving furiously as the truck sped away. On ahead, about 150 feet down the road, the truck spooked up four crows that had been gathered on the side of the road. As the birds flew up when the truck passed by, Mr. Shumple saw something fall to the ground and disappear in the dust that rose as the truck vanished into the distance.

Mr. Shumple moved on ahead into the settling dust down the road, and came upon what is was that had drawn the crows to that spot. Lying there in the rocks on the edge of the road were the partially consumed remains of a dead raccoon. It had not been there when Mr. Shumple had passed by that spot earlier that morning. It was the fresh product of road kill, but the hot midday sun had already done a number on the decaying corpse, and the scent was less than pleasant, even to Mr. Shumple. The tall grass and weeds growing in the ditch rustled, and inadvertently drew Mr. Shumple's attention. He peered into the weeds with his squinted eyes, searching for what might be moving in the brush - and then he saw.

Three of the black birds that had feasted on the raccoon had taken to the trees. One did not quite make it out from the reach of the pickup truck, and was knocked into the ditch, its left wing badly injured. Mr. Shumple cautiously approached it as it tried to flutter its way away from him.

"It's alright, little guy," he said aloud, although his tone would have been unconvincing had another human been in earshot of him. He was finally close enough to lunge at the wounded creature, and wrapped both hands firmly around the crow's body. He held tight enough so it could not break free from his hands, but not enough to cause it serious pain beyond that which it was already in with is broken wing.

Mr. Shumple took the crow back to his cart, and with one hand he tucked the crow under his arm as if it were a football, while with the other, he dumped the contents of one of the paper grocery bags from the market into another bag, and then placed the bird into the empty bag, rolling its top tightly closed. He held the rolled top of the bag in his hand, and with the hand that held the bag and his free hand, grasped both handles of his homemade rickshaw cart and continued down the road.

He was home within a half an hour, and before bringing his groceries inside the old shack, he brought the bag with the crow inside. Outside of the front door, a brown and gray stray cat, to which Mr. Shumple fed food scraps, paced back and forth anxiously as he approached, sniffing at the bag as he carried it by. The cat's fur was matted and dirty; Mr. Shumple pushed it aside with his foot as he passed into the house, slamming the door behind him. He looked around the small room, searching until he saw a large metal pail lying in the corner of the room. Mr. Shumple dragged the pail near the leg of an old fashioned school desk that he often ate his meals at, and then placed the rolled up paper bag atop the desk. He slowly and carefully unrolled the bag, laid it on its side, and reached in to grab the large bird.

  The bird barely fit inside the bag, and as soon as it was out, it desperately started to flutter its wings, both the good one and the injured one. Mr. Shumple held the bird by its neck, not so much to hurt it but to keep it still as he grabbed the large metal pail beside the desk and flipped it over, covering the bird on top of the desk.

  At first, there was no movement beneath the pail. Mr. Shumple stepped back a few feet and watched, as if he were waiting for something. He stood staring, narrowing his old eyes at the pail until suddenly it moved several inches across the desk. Mr. Shumple lurched forward and caught the pail just before the bird beneath shoved it off of the edge of the desk. He slid the pail back to the center of the desk, and quickly found a large rusty pipe wrench that was shoved between his electric stove and a cabinet in his tiny kitchen. He placed the wrench upon the pail, and he waited again. Moments later, the pail moved only a fraction of an inch. The weight of the heavy wrench seemed to be enough to hold down the injured crow. Mr. Shumple seemed satisfied.

  Just before Mr. Shumple crawled into his bed for the evening, he went around to the back of his shack where he had constructed a makeshift chicken pen, and filled a small trough full of chicken feed that he kept in a five gallon bucket just outside of the pen. Beside the pen, stretched across two galvanized metal saw horses, was what remained of a large oak door. The door had been cut in two, from top to bottom, and on the saw horses it had been tattered with dried blood and cut marks all across its surface. Only two chickens remained now, and they would suffice as meals for the next several days, provided the refrigerator kept the meat well after he slaughtered them. He would have to find a way to the Co-op to get more chickens soon, but for now, these two would be fine.

    A few hours into sleep, and into whatever it is a man like Mr. Shumple dreams, Mr. Shumple's rest was interrupted by the squawking and rustling of commotion coming from behind his home. He sprang up, much quicker than a man his age or overall condition would be expected to, grabbed a fireplace poker that he kept beneath the edge of his bed, and ran unknowingly and recklessly into the darkness behind the shack. When he was only a few feet from the chicken coop, the light from inside the kitchen that shown back into the coop through the open window revealed the reflected glare in the eyes of the two coyotes that had broken through the chicken wire that had easily kept the chickens in...but little to keep the larger, hungrier beasts out. Mr. Shumple screamed at the animals, who snarled back in return, and when one lunged toward him he swung out with his fireplace poker, just barely catching the nose of the coyote. The coyote let out a yelp, and retreated behind the other out of the hole they had made getting into the coop. Mr. Shumple retrieved a flashlight from inside the house and went to inspect the damage done to the coop. The fencing was badly mangled, and what remained of the two chickens appears to be a scattered mess of blood and feathers. He angrily struck the poker against one of the poles that held the fencing up, and went back into the shack - and back to a far more restless sleep until morning.

When Mr. Shumple awoke the next day, it was to the incessant caw of a large black crow perched on the open window over the chicken coop. He sat up and stared at the bird, and then looked at the pail on the small desk. The wrench was still firmly in place, and the pail did not look like it had been moved. He walked to the desk, and slowly lifted the edge of the pail. No sooner had he moved it, the bird inside began once again to flutter, this time more wildly and more desperately. When the crow under the pail began to do this, the one in the window began to caw more loudly than before, and yet another crow flew up to Mr. Shumple's front window, flapping its wings as if it were trying to push through the glass to get in. Startled by this, Mr. Shumple grabbed a book that was nearby and flung it in the direction of the crow in the kitchen window. He missed the bird by a long shot, but it was enough to get the bird to fly off away from the window. He rushed to the window and slammed it shut.

After eating the last few eggs from the coop, Mr. Shumple spent the next several hours securing and reinforcing the badly damaged fencing, driving more stakes into the ground around the coop and binding them tightly to the fence. The sun was hot that day as well, and he was feeling weary from the work. Weary, and hungry.

He came inside, sweaty and hot, and as much as he hoped for a breeze to come through and cool him, it did not come. The window was opened again, and as he sat for several minutes to collect himself and decide what he would do for a meal that evening, the large black crow from earlier had come back to the open window, once more cawing wildly. This time, Mr. Shumple himself jumped forward and went after the bird, which flew off in plenty of time before his fingertips grabbed the window and slammed it shut once more.

Then, an idea came to him. He looked at the pail on the desk, and lifted the wrench off that was weighing the pail down. Holding the edge of the bottom of the pail, he flung it from the desk and grabbed the bird by its neck before it could flutter off of the edge, and took the crow out the front door and around to the back of the shack. He held the bird down on the large oak door, and reached beneath the table, pulling an old and tarnished butcher knife from a wire milk crate. Holding the bird as steady as he could, he raised the large knife above his head. The crow that came twice to his window, and two more slightly smaller ones, cawed and stared at him as he held the knife up high. He saw the birds staring at him, and let an ever so subtle grin come to his lips as he brought the blade down upon the injured bird. The other birds let out a noise that Mr. Shumple thought, just for a moment, sounded like a human scream hidden deep within the natural voice of the cawing crows. The birds flew off together, and Mr. Shumple continued to prepare his meal.

    He didn't expect much from a scavenging creature such as this, but what he found gave him a very delightful surprise. It was unlike anything he had ever tasted before. He could feel a vibrancy in every bite, and with every morsel of the birds flesh. The taste itself was nothing all too special, but the unique surge of vitality he felt with every piece of meat was inexplicable. Mr. Shumple devoured the entire bird; every edible tidbit he could draw from its bones, and when he was finished, all he craved was *more*.

    He looked up from the remains of the carcass to see the large bird in the window again. It made no sound this time. It was just still, perched in the window with its head lowered and eyes fixed upon Mr. Shumple. Mr. Shumple felt a deep chill with the eyes of the crow upon him in this way. Before he could move a muscle, the bird turned and flew off on its own.

Mr. Shumple knew he wanted more. There had been nothing that he ever consumed that was anything like that bird. He needed more, and had to devise some clever way to get it. But these birds, uninjured, proved far to quick for him to catch. He needed something to draw them in, to get him within reach before they could get away. There was a scratching sound coming from the front door, and Mr. Shumple cautiously went to open it.

The stray cat stood there, looking up at him, and Mr. Shumple walked over to his table-desk and placed the dish with the crow's bones on the floor. The cat pranced in, and Mr. Shumple closed the door behind her, and watched the cat lick feverishly at the bones on the plate. He sat, and he watched, and yet another thought came to his hungry, twisted mind.

Sleep came and went with unsettling restlessness that night. The heat dissipated only a bit, and the cat knocked things about as she chased after the ever present mice that shared the home with Mr. Shumple. But it was mostly the ongoing churning of thoughts in his own head that kept Mr. Shumple from any sort of blissful slumber.

The sun rose early over the hills, and shone brightly through an east facing window that was coated with a thick layer of dust and housefly droppings. The cat anxiously paced back and forth near the front door of the shack. Mr. Shumple held his hand up in front of his face as he rose from the couch he laid upon that night, trying to cut the brightness that was filling the hot and muggy room. He looked towards the cat, and as he rose he picked up the fireplace poker that sat beside him on the floor next to the couch. He walked slowly to the door, eyeing the cat the whole way, and unlatched the door, opening it wide open with a quick thrust, allowing the light of outdoors to fill the otherwise dark and dingy room.

The cat stepped out only a few feet, and Mr. Shumple followed closely behind, keeping a close eye on the cat while also looking around in all directions, surveying the road and the surrounding area. He could not see, nor could he hear anything out of the ordinary. Birds chirped and tweeted in the distant trees, and there was once again no wind or even a slight breeze. It would be another sweltering day. The cat stepped forward a few more feet, and Mr. Shumple held the fireplace poker tightly in his left hand as he stepped up as well. He took one more glance around, up and down the road, and then looked down at the frazzled and tattered feline staring at the high grass ahead. Mr. Shumple slowly raised the poker in his left hand across his chest and high above his right shoulder, never taking his eyes off the cat, and swung down hard, striking the cat in the side of the head with a lethal blow that sent the animal spinning into the high grass that had caught its attention moments before.

Mr. Shumple shuddered for a moment. He had slaughtered plenty of chickens in his time, but he had never done anything like this before. It was the hunger inside of him that was his guiding force now, and it didn't take him long to overcome any feelings of revulsion he had at that moment.

Stepping quickly back to the house, he grabbed a fishing net with green netting and scooped the up cat carcass. He started to head up the road in the direction away from town, farther from where people may find themselves traveling. He walked for nearly twenty-five minutes until he found a spot that he deemed suitable. The grass and weeds were high along the sides of the road. The tree-line started several yards away from the edge of the road, back behind the high weeds. Another 300 feet further up the road was the edge of a grassy field that went on for several miles that used to be active farm land. Mr. Shumple believed that it wouldn't take long for the scavenging black devils to find the dead cat, and to make it their feast. And he would be there, watching and waiting.

Mr. Shumple dumped the cat from the net, just along the edge of the weed line, and crawled into the high grass five or six feet back. There he stayed, watching and waiting as the minutes went by...and then an hour. The heat was rising, and Mr. Shumple found himself restless and anxious. He was irritated, and he was hungry. He had not eaten anything before he murdered the cat. His mind was focused only on his mission, and he knew that his hunger would only cause him to savor the next bird that much more. No cars had passed by in that hour. It had been deathly quiet, until finally, he heard a familiar cawing in the distance.

Mr. Shumple narrowed his eyes as the first bird came within a few feet of the cat. Then he watched two others come out of nowhere and land near the animal as well. The three crows came upon the cat and started picking and pecking at the matted body. Mr. Shumple clenched the handle of his net tighter and found his footing, readying himself to launch from the grass to capture his prey. He pushed himself forward with blinding conviction, and slammed down with the net on the banquet of crows, landing belly down in the dust as well.

His face lay in the gravel for several seconds, and when his eyes rose to view his catch, he found that he had only captured the dead cat once more in his net. He let out a growl of anger, and then out of the corner of his eye he saw up the road a figure of a man approaching. He stared off in the direction of the man, trying to focus, then dropped his head back to the gravel and waited.

Mr. Shumple stared in silence as the man got closer. The approaching man was tall, wearing jeans and a white t-shirt with the sleeves cut off. The man's skin was dark and deeply tanned, and his features and long black ponytail strongly revealed his Native American heritage. Along side him walked his German Shepherd. The dog's name was Max, and the man's name was John Worthweather.

John lived another half mile up the road, and operated a taxidermy shop out of his home. He was in his mid-fifties, and one of the only other people who lived in these outskirts of town. Also, he was one of the only people around that actually talked to Mr. Shumple. He did not fear the man like others did, and was not easily intimidated either. It should not be said that Mr. Shumple liked John Worthweather, nor did Worthweather like Mr. Shumple. However, John treated Mr. Shumple with respect, and for the most part, that respect was returned by Mr. Shumple's in his own way. John was not afraid to call things as he saw them, and whatever this was that Mr. Shumple was up to was not going to go without inquiry.

"What the hell are you up to, Otis?" asked John, looking down at the odd scene. Very few people knew Mr. Shumple's first name. Precisely, very few cared, but John had lived in the area all of his life and he knew many things of the people that lived in his home town.

Mr. Shumple looked up from the dust, and began to push his way up off of the gravel.

"It's none of your damn business, Worthweather," Mr. Shumple snarled back at him.

John looked at the cat on the road, as the dog sniffed at the remains. He looked at the net, as Mr. Shumple lifted it from the ground, and at the same moment the caws of the crows from the trees drew his attention. John looked up at the three birds perched in the surrounding trees, and looked back at Mr. Shumple as he picked himself up and brushed some of the dust from his clothing and face.

John had a sharp eye, and a sharp mind as well. He had been around and knew many things, and it did not take him long to figure out what Mr. Shumple was up to.

"You don't want to be doing this, Shumple," John told him in a stern voice.

"I told you to mind your own business," Mr. Shumple growled again, but would not look John in the eye when he said it.

John looked down at him for a moment, and then looked off into the distance up the road. He looked back down at the cat in the rocky sand, and took notice of the wound on the cat's head, knowing full and well this was not a victim of road kill, but something else entirely.

"Nature makes a waste of nothing, Otis," said John, looking back into the distance. "It's man that is selfish and wasteful, and it is man that disrupts the balance of things. Every creature under the sun has a purpose. And as such, every creature should be treated with the deepest respect. That is what I try to do in my business. When I make a mount, I am doing what I can to honor the body *and* the spirit that once inhabited the animals remains."

"Do you have a point?" snapped Mr. Shumple, seeming more and more agitated.

"The crows...they have a purpose as well, and it is unwise to disrupt the balance of nature. Many people look at these birds as the custodians of the roadways, cleaning up and putting to use what man has so recklessly destroyed and disregarded. But many years ago, my grandmother told me what she believed about these birds. She told me that all animals have a spirit self, and when their lives are cut short before their time, the spirits of these animal might get trapped inside of their bodies. The crows would come to these poor creatures, and as they would consume the remains, they would take the lost spirits of the animals as well, and then the crows would carry the spirits on to whatever place that the spirits go on to."

    Mr. Shumple still would not look John in the eye, and held his scowl firmly upon his face.

    "Do what you will, Otis," John said with a sigh, turning back in the direction he came. "But if you were to ask me....it is not a good idea to tamper with the balance of things. Those meant to consume who are the carriers of souls are not meant to be consumed themselves. It is a cycle that man shouldn't be a part of. Man has, after all, done enough damage."

    John looked once more at the bludgeoned cat, and continued along his way. Mr. Shumple stood along side the road until John disappeared into the distance, and his mind went right back to finding a way to get his hands on another crow. He cared nothing for John's words or old wives tales. John didn't *know*...he didn't know the feeling. If he were to feast upon one himself, he would understand. Mr. Shumple scooped the cat up once more, and brought it into the tall grass where he had been lying in wait for the crows. He dug a hole with his hands, large enough to bury the cat so the crows wouldn't find it. He came to realize that the only way that he could get close enough to catch a crow was if the crows came right upon *himself*. He decided the only way to do this was to play dead and draw the birds in. He would lie upon the roadside, and he would wait. And when the birds came to him...to try and feast on his flesh...then he would have them!

Another hour had gone by as Mr. Shumple laid in the dust beside the road, about fifty yards away from where the cat had laid. The midday sun was at its peak, and the heat was beginning to make Mr. Shumple feel ill. But the focus of his fevered agenda caused him to disregard common wisdom to abandon his course that day, return to his home, and drink a cold glass of water. He would go to whatever length it would take to capture his prey, even though it never occurred to the old man to wonder why he truly wanted it so bad. All he knew was...he must have it.

Moments later, he heard the flutter of wings nearby, and out of the corner of his squinted eyes he could see the large crow drawing cautiously closer. His excitement had ignited, and it was all he could do to remain still as the bird hopped closer to his outstretched hand. Then, he could hear it coming on up the road...it was the sound of a vehicle barreling in his direction. All day long, there had not been one car or truck on this road, and now, with victory within his reach, here one came.

He remained still as the tan sedan came to a stop right where he laid. The crow had disappeared without his notice while he had become overtaken with anger by the approach of the vehicle. The car's door opened, and a man in denim shorts and a muscle shirt ran over to Mr. Shumple as he lie on the ground.

"Mister! Can you hear me? Don't worry...I'll call for help," the man said frantically. He had gotten close enough to Mr. Shumple that Mr. Shumple easily, and very surprisingly to the young man, clenched the man's arm that held his cell phone and stared with a fiery look in his eyes at the man.

"Do you know what you've DONE? Get out of here! Get out of here NOW or I'll feed you to those damn birds myself!"

The man's eyes widened and a look of terror came upon his face. No sooner had Mr. Shumple released his grip did the man pull away, almost tripping as he scuttled back to his car door and took off down the road. The anger was so great in Mr. Shumple that he felt his heart pounding in his chest as he tried to calm himself and lie still once more, hoping the crows would soon return.

Just as the dust settled from the car that sped away, and largest of the crows did return. Mr. Shumple could see him plainly, and somehow he knew that this was the crow that perched in his window, screaming at him when he still had the other one trapped beneath the bucket. It moved closer, and then lowered its head as it did after Mr. Shumple had fed upon the other crow. As the large bird stared at him while he lied still in the gravel, two more crows came down from the nearby trees, and Mr. Shumple could feel once more his anxiousness growing. The largest crow crept closer by only a few inches, and his heart began to race...until...the pain gripped him in his chest.

Mr. Shumple's hand flew up from his side, grasping at the center of his chest as the pain moved down his arm, and soon enveloped his whole body. He couldn't breath, and he could no longer move, and despite the sudden spasms that had overtaken him for those few moments, the crows had not budged or been spooked away. They stood by and watched this man writhe and then go still, and saw the glaze form over his still open eyes. Mr. Shumple himself, while overtaken with the pain and now lying motionless, was completely aware of everything around him. He could see everything. He could hear everything, including the sound of his heart beating its final beats before going completely silent. Most significantly, Mr. Shumple could *feel* everything.

Soon, several more crows descended around his body, and all he could do now was watch as three became seven...and then ten...and then more than he could see or count around him. The crows inched closer, and it was the big one that came up upon his chest and stared into his glazed over eyes; and now, Mr. Shumple knew. He knew the fear that the injured bird had when Mr. Shumple held it captive, intending it for his meal. He now had felt what the bird had felt in its final moments before Mr. Shumple brought the blade down upon it; but it was not going to be so quick and easy for Otis Shumple.

All too late did the full meaning of John Worthweather's words come to light in Mr. Shumple's stubborn and hunger driven mind. The bird he had eaten carried part of the soul of the dead raccoon, and when he tasted the flesh of the bird, he had also tasted the soul of the creature the crow carried with it - a taste that was never intended for any living creature. A burst of energy and wonder at the cost of another's soul was an abomination of nature, and as for such a thing, a steep price must be paid.

Even after the life had left his body, Otis Shumple was overtaken with terror as the whole gathering of crows came upon him at once, ravaging the flesh of his physical remains. He felt everything...every peck and pull and tear that each crow took from him...and only when the crows were finished with him would his own soul be set free. Such was the penance of this misguided and unfortunate man.

As the years passed, people would tell the story of the old man that John Worthweather had found along the road the following day; or rather, what was left of the man. Never had there been a case of a man so quickly and cleanly picked to the bone by any scavenging creatures around. The authorities were baffled, but John would tell the story as a warning to any and all intending to disrespect the laws and ways of nature. And to those who would go wandering those roads, exploring the legend of old Mr. Shumple, some would find that his soul did not wander far. He has been seen on late nights, wandering the roads in flashes of headlights and glimpses of shadow. And there are those that have claimed to hear his cries in the winds that whisper through the trees; a cry echoed in the familiar sounds of the cawing crows that rest upon their limbs, watching over the roadways of the souls forgotten...

Rick Jurewicz

Once Upon a Wicked Eve

The Pale-Faced Man
A Halloween Tale

"What time are you meeting the other boys?" Billy's mother called out to Billy from the kitchen.

"Zach said we were gonna meet at 5:30," Billy called back, hurriedly putting the final touches on the make-up for his costume. He decided for his costume this year he was going to go out as Count Dracula. Ever boy needs to be Dracula at least once. It was classic, and Count Dracula was a symbol of the true dark origins of the vampire legend, back when the blood-sucking fiends were still cool and didn't sparkle in the sunlight. He wasn't sure about doing it at first, but his mom coaxed him into it. After he started getting the costume together - the long black cape and the cool, real-looking fangs - it was all he wanted to be. Billy was 12 years old now, and this could be the last Halloween that he was going to go out trick-or-treating, so he wanted to make it a good one.

Billy's mother was finishing up the dishes when she heard the dog starting to bark from the back yard near the fence alongside the house. Kibbles was a poodle mix; mixed with what, no one was sure. He had a classic little-dog complex, barking at every little thing that came by the house in an effort to show everyone how tough and fearless he was. This would not go well on Halloween, whether they kept him inside the house or out. It was rare for random passersby to come close enough to the house to get Kibbles' attention in a small town subdivision like the one Billy Blake lived in, but the smaller children had already started coming up and down the road begging for treats, and that was more than enough to set Kibbles off.

"Billy," his mother called out once more. "Do you need a ride somewhere? Where are you meeting the others?"

"We're gonna meet at the library," Billy called back. He was finished and ready. Fangs were in place and ready to chomp unsuspecting victims in the night...as well as the candy too, of course. Can't forget chomping the candy. "I don't need a ride. I can walk." *What self respecting 12 year old wants to be seen with their parents on Halloween?*

"Okay. But I need you to take Kibbles out and put him in the garage for a few hours. Give him food and water, and turn on your dad's TV for him. It'll keep him company."

"Okay Mom, I will! See you later!" Billy yelled as the front slammed behind him.

Zach Garritt walked along the main street sidewalk, stopping in front of the Native Springs Public Library. He sat down on the bench that was in front of the library, watching the kids walk by. He saw Batman and Spider-man, at least 3 Harry Potters, and an endless line of zombies and princesses.

Zach spent the better half of the afternoon wrapping himself in long white strips of old sheets his mother helped him cut. Dad helped him wrap the strips for a while before he had to leave for his evening shift on the Native Springs Police Department. Halloween always had a few extra patrols for both safety reasons and keeping as eye out for mischievous teens looking for some destructive fun. It was usually eggs thrown on cars, soap on storefront windows, and the occasional case of a public fountain loaded with sudsy laundry detergent. Nothing real damaging, just enough to annoy the authorities and a few residents.

The costume turned out looking great, although it did tend to make it a little difficult to move in certain ways, and Zach was beginning to think sitting down was not the best idea. He was afraid that he was going to rip the sheets, so he sat there and waited for reinforcements.

A few minutes went by before a black, two-door Buick Riviera pulled up. The passenger, a teenage girl with black, curly hair, wearing a beat up leather motorcycle jacket, got out of the front seat to let Frankenstein's Monster out of the black seat of the car.

"Have fun, Stevie," said the girl as she got back into the car. The Riviera pulled away from the curb.

"Thank's for the ride, Jake!" Stevie Stratton yelled, waving as the car pulled up Main Street. There was a honk of the horn and a wave out of the driver's side window as the car drove out of sight.

Stevie's costume looked great as well, with the squared-up head that seemed seamless as it met his face. The skin was green and the bolts in his neck looked real.

"That is awesome!" said Zach.

"My dad helped a lot. This was his favorite costume when he was a kid. Where is Taylor?" asked Stevie.

From behind the shrub nearest the bench leapt the creature, snarling and ferocious. It was covered in brown hair from head to foot, wearing an old flannel shirt and torn-up jeans. Stevie spun around as Zach jumped up from the bench, tearing a few sheet strips in the process.

The creature began to laugh hysterically at the two boys, who stood wide-eyed with fright.

"You should see the looks on your faces right now!" exclaimed the creature, whose lips did not move when he spoke or laughed.

"Dammit, Taylor!" yelled Zach. "You made me rip my mummy bandages!"

It didn't seem to phase Taylor. He kept on laughing at his friend. Stevie helped tuck the loose bandages out of the way so Zach wouldn't completely unravel.

"Nice werewolf costume, Taylor," said Stevie. The head was a full pullover mask that was incredibly realistic, and the hands and feet were both covered in fur.

"Thanks, Stevie," said Taylor, who finally stopped laughing. "Hey, where's your sister tonight?"

"She went out with Jake. They just dropped me off before you popped out."

"I missed her? She is so hot!" said Taylor, who followed his comment with a howl like a wolf at the still invisible moon.

Stevie rolled his eyes, but said nothing. He looked up the sidewalk to see the vampire making his way up the street.

Billy walked up to the three other boys waiting for him. He had a huge smile with jutting fangs on his face. Stevie was the first to notice the fangs in his mouth.

"Those look so real," Stevie said enthusiastically.

"They are real," said Billy. The words came out a bit awkwardly. Billy found it was a bit difficult to talk normal with the fake fangs in his mouth.

"Alright. Let's get this show on the road! This is gonna be our last Halloween trick-or-treat night before we are teenagers. Let's get our candy, boys!" roared the wolf-boy Taylor.

As the boys started up the street away from the library, Stevie stopped and stared between the two building across the street from the library.

"Hey...guys. Look at that." He pointed to the wooded area in the distance between the two buildings. Just behind the tree line, the four of them made out the pale shape of a face staring in their direction. It was motionless, and without expression - a mask of a human face.

"Is that a person? Or is that a decoration?" asked Zach, not able to take his eyes off of the figure.

"It's not moving," said Taylor. "It's probably just a prop or something someone put there to freak people out."

"It's working," said Billy. He stood transfixed upon the cold glare of the black eyes in the distance. "Come on. Let's just go, okay?"

Without a word, the boys moved on, each slowly turning away from the face in the trees. They continued to the next block before turning down the well populated Parker Street.

As the night continued on, the boys hit up almost every house in the downtown area. When they got to the corner of Patterson and Green Streets, Taylor stopped dead in his tracks. He stood frozen, peering into the darkness beyond the last lit house lights on Patterson Street. Zach saw Taylor stop, and looked to see what it was that caused his friend to go still. The other two boys followed suit, and quickly saw the same face they had seen earlier in the night, pale-white and stone-like.

The porch lights of the nearby houses reflected dimly on the smooth features of the mask. In the eyes there was only blackness. Framing the cold face was a black hood over the head and draped down to the shoulders. The figure was closer now by half the distance it was when they had seen it earlier. It was wearing a long, charcoal grey coat that disappeared into the darkness at its feet. It did not make the slightest movement.

Each of the four boys could feel a chill run through them. Zach and Stevie looked to each other. They were the best of friends, and could often tell what each other was thinking. But at that moment, neither boy knew what to think or say. They were scared, but as often, most 12 year old boys never want to admit to being afraid. They looked to Green Street, the least lit street in the downtown area. Only one porch light was lit, and no other cars were down that street. They could turn back, but turning back only meant staying in the back streets longer, while cutting up Green Street was the most direct way back to Main Street, where there were still loads of people going from storefront to storefront getting treats.

"Come on," Taylor said, turning to walk up Green Street.

Billy, Zach and Stevie followed behind. All of the boys quickened their pace. None of them dared look back to see if the figure was coming up behind them. They focused their attention on the one lit house, like it was a beacon of safe harbor to a ship lost at sea.

When they finally came to the edge of the yard, they were surprised to see how well decorated the house and yard were. They couldn't see from so far away, but up close, it was a wonderful surprise.

The driveway and garage were dark, but the yard to the small cabin-like house was strewn with spider-webs covering the shrubs along the edge of the yard, and artificial black cats were all around different corners of the yard. There was a tall, menacing scarecrow propped at the corner of the driveway with a creepy raven set upon its shoulder.

The pathway to the front door was lined with jack-o-lanterns illuminated with real candles, six on each side of the path. The boys could see an old woman through the large window on the porch watching television. The living room was lit with only one lamp and the light of the TV set. On the porch, silhouetted against the living room window, stood the life-sized shape of a witch.

The boys, standing completely still, stared at the witch shape, which was equally motionless. Finally, the witch shifted its position and a voice came from the darkened porch.

"Well, come on up," said the voice of the witch.

The boys cautiously moved forward, Zach taking the lead. Stevie followed behind Zach first, then Taylor and Billy, side by side. As they got closer to the porch, the witch stepped into the light of the orange bulb on the porch. They could see now that the witch they had all been afraid of was actually Mrs. Crawford, the boys old elementary school secretary.

"Are you boys having a nice time tonight? You're staying out of trouble, right?" she asked the boys, looking each one up and down as if she was measuring them to see if they were being naughty that night.

"Hi, Mrs. Crawford," said Stevie. "Trick or treat!"

"Stevie Stratton," she replied, smiling. "If all of this group is with you, I am sure you are all staying out of trouble." She put a handful of candy into each one of the boys bags. "Not many kids venture down this street. Too dark for most. What brought you four down here?"

At first, the boys said nothing. Finally, Billy spoke up.

"There was this man. I mean...we think it was a man. We saw him a couple of times tonight. He was just staring at us. He didn't move. He didn't say anything. He just stared. It kind of...well..."

"He scared you," she stated. "It's okay to feel scared. It is Halloween, after all. But there are ways to protect yourselves on Halloween. Do you know why people dress up in costumes on this night?"

"Umm," started Taylor. "Isn't it to get candy?"

"Yes," she said, sitting down on her porch step. "But do you know how it started?"

The boys stood in silence. Slowly each began to shake there heads from side to side.

"In ancient times, in the Celtic lands of Ireland, Scotland and Great Britain, there was a time at the end of the summer after the harvest, called Samhain. With the coming of winter just around the corner, there were celebrations and sometimes, sacrifices. The people believed that during this time, long before it became the American tradition of Halloween, that the boundary between the world of the living and the world of the dead was thin and could easily be passed through by the recently deceased. People wore disguises around this time to hide from evil or vengeful spirits that may come seeking to do harm. They often would dress themselves as these spirits to throw them off and blend in. The food and the fun came later."

"You know a lot about Halloween, Mrs. Crawford," said Zach.

"It's my favorite holiday, Mr. Garritt," she told him, grinning widely, "I think someone is just trying to have some fun with you tonight. If it was a spirit, your costumes should keep you safe. Even the spirits can disguise themselves on Halloween. Perhaps it is just one, trying to have some fun of its own. By the way, I love all of the classic movie monsters you boys dressed up as. All anyone ever sees anymore are zombies, princesses, or zombie-princesses."

The boys looked at each other, only now for the first time realizing what they had done. Each one had thought that they were coming up with something original for a costume. Something completely on their own. Stevie's mother came up with Frankenstein after she had talked to Zach's mother, and Billy's mom got wind of the idea and called Taylor's dad. It took little coaxing. Zach was sure that there would be a lot of laughs had about it and pictures taken when his mother picked them up later that night.

"It's not that far to Main Street from here. Did you guys want me to walk you up there?" asked Mrs. Crawford.

"No," said Taylor. The word came quick from his lips. He knew that if any other people from his class saw them walking the streets with the elementary secretary, they would never hear the end of it at school. Something like that could haunt them forever.

"Okay then. Well, you boys have a nice night. Happy Halloween!" she exclaimed as the boys walked down the path away from the house. Billy turned around and went back to Mrs. Crawford on the porch. The other three boys stopped and looked back, wondering what he was doing.

Mrs. Crawford leaned in to Billy.

"What's on your mind, Billy Blake?" she asked him.

"Mrs. Crawford...I hope you don't get mad for me asking this. That stuff you said about Halloween. Do you...do you know that because...are you a real witch? It's just...I've heard things..."

Mrs. Crawford smiled. "I know. Yes, I am a real witch. But not the kind you think of, dressed like this and flying around on brooms. I believe in a deeper connection with nature. There are many old ways and old beliefs. But I am a good witch. And as far as that stuff that I know about Halloween? I read. It's a good habit to get into."

Billy nodded his head to her, and turned back to walk with the other boys.

"What was that all about?" Mrs. Crawford could hear one of the boys say as they disappeared into the darkness up Green Street on the way back to Main Street. It was then she looked up and saw the same figure the boys had seen that night, just on the other side of the street. It did not look in her direction. It was standing facing the boys as they moved up the street, but the figure did not follow them, at least not in a way that the eye could detect motion.

"Oh dear," she whispered to herself, bowing her head. When she raised her head back up, the figure was no where to be seen. She looked around her yard, and she could neither hear nor see anyone else around. She walked to each jack-o-lantern and knelt down beside it, and with a sharp blow, extinguished each one before returning to her porch to shut off the last light of the evening. Green Street was left to the darkness of the night.

The boys made it back to Main Street without any problem. Zach's mother was to meet them in a half an hour back at the library to take them back to Zach's house for a night of spooky movies and popcorn.

"Let's try and hit up some of the businesses again on Main Street. They can't remember everyone that has come through already," said Taylor.

Zach shrugged. "Sound's good to me. We can just head back toward the library."

"Guys...I don't feel so good. I think I am going to go home," said Billy.

"What's wrong?" asked Stevie.

"Nothing...I mean, I just don't feel good."

"Come on, Billy. Shake it off. There's more candy to be had," burst out Taylor.

"Do you need us to walk you home?" asked Zach.

"No. I'll be fine. I just need to go home," Billy said, turning to walk in the opposite direction.

"If you change your mind, have your mom call my mom, or just come on over. We'll be up late," said Zach.

"Okay," said Billy, stopping only for a moment to answer them before continuing down the street.

"Well, more candy for us then," Taylor stated, and howled once more into the sky, which was still moonless.

The remaining three boys continued towards the library. The girl at the convenience store giving out full cans of pop recognized the boys, but still smiled and gave them an extra can each.

"Here," she said. "Take one for your friend. Count Dracula. Where is he?"

All of the heads at the convenience store turned when they heard the echoing sounds and saw the flashing lights of an ambulance and police car far up the street, turning several blocks away from where they were now. They didn't think much about it, really. The three boys started up to the library once again, but they only made it about 50 feet before a yellow SUV pulled up beside them on the street. The passenger side and rear door of the SUV opened.

The boys were startled by the sudden arrival of the vehicle. It was Taylor's dad's SUV. He was behind the steering wheel. Taylor's mom got out of the front. The rear door was open, and sitting in the back of the vehicle was Zach's mother. She was visible upset, but she did not say anything. Taylor's mother approached the boys. When she got closer to them, the boys could tell she had been crying.

"Mom...what's wrong?" Taylor asked. His voice was quivering. The snarky, candy driven kid he had been throughout the night was no longer anywhere to be seen.

"Boys," she paused, searching for composure. "You need to come with us. There was...an accident."

Zach looked to his mother in the back seat. "My dad...is he alright?"

"Not your dad, Zach," said Taylor's mother. "It's Billy."

Taylor's father drove them all back to Zach's home where they waited almost another 45 minutes for Zach's father to pull into the driveway with his squad car. He came in to the house, and was immediately embraced by Zach's mother, who broke down in tears.

The boys had said nothing to each other or anyone else since they had been picked up on the street. They just sat beside one another looking down at their candy bags. Zach held the extra can of pop meant for Billy in his hand.

"Do they know what happened?" asked Taylor's dad.

"Billy's mother found him in their garage," said Zach's dad. "There was nothing they could do."

"I knew we should have walked him home," said Zach, under his breath.

"What are you talking about, sweetie?" asked Zach's mother.

"He said that he didn't feel good. I asked him if he wanted us to walk him home. He said no. We should have walked him home. What happened to him? Was it that guy?" asked Zach.

"What guy?" asked Taylor's dad.

"We kept on seeing this guy all night," said Stevie. "He wore a white mask and a hood. A long coat. We kept seeing him. Did he...did he do something to hurt Billy?"

"No," said Zach's dad. "Nobody killed Billy. His heart. It just stopped. His mother found him in the garage when she went out to let the dog in. Zach, you said you saw Billy tonight. When did you see him?"

"He was with us all night trick-or-treating. He left us to go home 15 minutes before you guys pulled up. We should have went with him!" Zach was angry and upset.

The adults in the room looked around to each other. There was a glazed over look of confusion on their faces. Zach's father knelt down in front of Zach and the other two boys, who were sitting still in shock.

"Zach," he said softly, looking at his son. "You said he was out with you tonight. That's not possible. When his mother sent him out to put the dog in the garage late this afternoon, he never came out again. At least not until the paramedics took him out. He...he was in full rigor mortis. He'd already been dead for hours, son."

Zach, Stevie and Taylor all looked up at Zach's dad, then around the room at the others.

Taylor looked at his father, and then to his mother.

"He was with us. All night. I swear," Taylor said.

Zach held up the can of pop in his hand. "The girl. At the convenience store. When we went back to get more pop, she asked about him. She remembered him from earlier. She gave this to me to give to him. *To Count Dracula*, she said. We didn't know he was going to be Count Dracula. It was a surprise. When they found him...what was he dressed as? Was he Count Dracula for Halloween, Dad?"

Zach's father held a pale, blank stare on his face. Every eye in the room was on him. He traced all of their faces with his eyes before giving an almost imperceptible nod of his head.

The funeral for Billy was held 7 days later, and it was the largest that the town had seen for quite some time. The boys did not speak of the night of trick-or-treating with each other, or with anyone else, after that night. With one exception.
At the burial, Zach saw Mrs. Crawford alone in the distance outside of the parting crowd. He left his parents and ran out toward her, catching up with her near her car.
"Mrs. Crawford!" Zach yelled, almost out of breath.
She turned to Zach and tilted her head subtly.
"I'm sorry about your friend, Mr. Garritt," she told Zach.
"Mrs. Crawford, I need to ask you a question," Zach told her.
"Alright. Go ahead."
"I've heard the rumors too. About you. The...the witch stuff. When we were at your house, you saw him. Billy. You talked to him. Did you know?"
"Know what? That he was a ghost? No. I didn't."
Zach lowered his chin down, and looked at the ground. Mrs. Crawford put her hand on his shoulder and knelt down in front of Zach.
"I did know, soon after, that something had gone terribly wrong that night. When I saw the man you boys spoke of. He was watching you as you walked away. And I knew. I just didn't know who."
"You saw him? Who was he?"

She fixed her eyes on Zach's, and gave him the most serious look that he had ever seen her give anyone in all the years he'd known her.

"Billy died on the night when the barrier between this life and the next was at its thinnest. And he was in disguise, hiding from the spirits of the netherworld. Death came for him, and at first, Billy slipped though his fingers. But even on Halloween, when all things play dress up and nothing is as it seems...*Death* was never far behind."

Rick Jurewicz

They Say it Happened

The narrow and heavily overgrown two-track ended abruptly in a twisted mess of large, jagged-edged rocks and the remnants of old trees long since dead and fallen. The trees themselves had much of their own new growth sprouting forth from them; patches of moss and newly sprouted saplings popping up and reaching toward whatever sunlight they could find.

"What now?" asked Lisa from the rear seat in the old minivan. She was sweating more than anyone else in the van. The air conditioning didn't reach the back of the van very well, and the other four teens in the van did not want to open the windows and let out what little cool air they could muster from the overworked air conditioning unit.

"Now, we walk the rest of the way," answered Jill from the front passenger seat.

This had been Jill's idea from the beginning, a last-blast of summer before senior year outing for the little group of horror fanatics and lovers of all things supernatural. They created their own private club, and it consisted of Jill and Lisa, along with Jill's boyfriend Matt and Matt's brother Jay. The most recent addition to the club was Angela, who wasn't from the same high school as the rest of the gang, but came from a neighboring town and met Jill while working together at a local kayak and tube rental business as a summer job.

Angela started out quiet, helping load and unload kayaks before and after trips down the Sturgeon River. Jill worked behind the counter at the gift shop. One day Angela came to work and didn't have time to change into her work shirt before she got to the store. She walked in wearing a t-shirt for the movie "The Grudge", and Jill almost immediately knew she was a kindred spirit. They struck up a conversation about the movie and Angela's love for horror films and books, and before Jill knew it, Angela went from almost total silence to talking like an out of control machine gun.

Jill introduced her to the rest of the group shortly after, and the rest of the summer they spent watching spooky movies and talking about new ones that had come out at the theater that summer. They enjoyed discussing what ideas they might embark on for Halloween in the coming fall, and even had a few nights where they snuck into local cemeteries in the middle of the night wandering around just to see if they could scare each other – and themselves.

In this day and age, true fans of the horror genre find it hard to actually find something that truly scares them. Today was something new for them all, and the hopes were high that something frightening would find them all on this last-blast outing into the deep woods northeast of Native Springs, the small northern town that Matt, Jay, Jill and Lisa had grown up in together.

It was Angela's idea at first, at least in the sense that she was the first one to tell Jill the stories and rumors she had heard about the area they were about to enter. They all knew about this road, and they had all been here before on late nights over the past couple of years. It was this spot where they were now parked, down a long and twisted single two-track, that came to be known as "Billy's Tomb".

Billy's Tomb was a classic local urban legend story about a young boy named Billy who had lived in the early 1900s. It was said that on the morning of his 8th birthday, Billy woke up well before anyone else in his house. His parents were still fast asleep, and his two younger sisters, six-year-old Clara and four-year old Carol – still in a deep sleep as well - shared a room beside Billy's just down the hall from their parents bedroom.

Billy's parent awoke and found Billy in the kitchen eating a biscuit at the breakfast table. Billy was covered in blood, and his mother ran to him and started looking him over to see where he had hurt himself.

"It's not from me, Mama," Billy said without any notable expression on his face.

His mother looked back over her shoulder at her husband, and a feeling of panic ran between them. Billy's father ran to the girls' bedroom, and the horrible scream that followed echoed through the tiny farmhouse.

It is said that Billy's father, who loved his son more than life itself, buried the girls in a far spot off the edge of a nearby field, deep in the ground. Billy's mother fell into a deep depression, never leaving the house, and rarely leaving the room where her two little girls fell into a forever sleep by the blade of the razor that had been in Billy's hand. Billy and his father would often hear her talking to the sisters as if she were in conversation with them. Sometimes she would laugh, sometimes she would cry, and then finally one day no sounds came from the room at all.

Billy's father could not find Billy or his mother upon returning from the fields that day, finally coming to look in the room where the girls had died.

Billy sat in the corner of the room, cross-legged with his eyes fixed upon his mother, who hung by the neck from a rope affixed to an open wooden beam in the ceiling.

In a fit of hysterics, Billy's father grabbed his shotgun from his bedroom and dragged his son to a place just west of the tree line, beyond the sight of the little farmhouse where they had made their home. Believing the boy had the Devil in him, he made Billy dig a hole more than six feet into the ground. As the boy stood in the hole he had just dug, Billy's father took aim with the shotgun, and through tears streaming down his face, he pulled the trigger, killing his son.

He then buried Billy in the hole and brought large rocks from the nearby field to mark the grave, not as a remembrance, but as a warning to those who wandered this way of the evil that once flourished on these lands.

After the deed was done, Billy's father walked alone back to his house. He sat down on the front porch swing, put the barrel of the shotgun in his mouth and pulled the trigger.

Or so the story goes.

Angela and Jill found the story was full of holes. No one who ever researched the story could find a record of the family existing in this area. And this road at one time in the last 70 years actually did lead to somewhere, so the rocks were placed here at a later time. But that didn't stop decades of teens from driving out for a thrill to the place that came to be called Billy's Tomb. And more than half swear they have had any number of strange occurrences happen upon visiting this place. Car engines mysteriously stalled. Headlamps blink on and off without anyone causing them to. And many believe when they sat in silence at this spot, they could hear the screams of the young sisters in the distant woods surrounding the place of the "grave". Some even believed they saw eerie lights across the distant horizon through the trees.

    This group of teens had all been here before, they'd all heard the stories and done their own paranormal investigations, and came to realize that the stories were all just a bunch of crap. That was not what brought them here today. Today, it was another story of something that they DID find in the record books and newspaper clippings that happened back in these woods in the summer of 1956.

    The five of them got out of the van, each carrying a backpack with items that Jill prescribed for them to bring along. Lisa's was simple – snacks and water for everyone. Jay's pack was and largest, as he was the biggest person in the group that could carry the heaviest load. His pack was filled with candles, a small fire extinguisher, audio recording devices and a couple of mini rechargeable video cameras. Jill carried a couple of books about hauntings that she took almost everywhere she went. Also, she carried a more basic supply of items that included insect repellant, a first-aid kit, flashlights and a couple of flares. Angela had what she believed were items that could protect the group from harm if in fact they did find a malevolent spirit in tow. This included a small vial of holy water taken from the water pool of a local Catholic church, crosses, a bible, and a small statuette of St. Peter.

    Matt was assigned to carry the thing Jill held most important and precious to the evenings activities – her hand-made Ouija board. The board had been cut and carved from an old maple block that her grandfather had made, and it was Jill that found it in her grandfather's garage after he died and refinished the surface and hand-painted the board herself. Her grandfather was the first person she tried to contact with the board once she had finished it, and she swears to have spoken to him through the board that day.

Despite the heavy heat in the air, the afternoon sun was fading fast. They started off walking in the direction that the old road had taken, even though it was at times hard to discern what had been road and what had become random treks through the woods. There were a few times that they had found their way off of the road, but with a little searching for the right signs — certain rock formations along the edge of the old road and a distinct difference in the size of trees along the pathway — they found the way once more.

"So what is the story about this place again?" asked Jay, who had only heard the story once before. He had been out of town when Angela and Jill discovered the story while further researching the tales about Billy's Tomb. It was an accident, really. A plat map of the area that might have been able to tell the family name that Billy could be connected to pointed in a direction that they had not at all seen coming.

"A traveling circus had come to the area for an extended amount of time back in the 1950s. It traveled by train right through this area before all of the tracks were pulled up back in the 80s. This was at one time all farm land, and for some unknown reason these fields were no longer producing good crops. The farmer was offered what was a generous sum at the time by the circus to set up shop here for an undetermined amount of time," Jill explained.

Angela took over the tale. "The story almost seemed kind of clichéd, so at first we didn't really believe what was said to have taken place, but the further we dug into it, we discovered newspaper clippings that confirmed the story. There was…"

"Don't tell me," Jay interrupted. "A crazy clown." He smirked, but the girls just gave him a look like he had wandered onto forbidden ground cutting them off from the telling of their tale.

"Yes," Jill continued. "But he was driven that way by jealousy. By all accounts from the surviving witnesses, Cindertop the Clown was a really friendly guy, helping around the circus wherever he could when the make-up was off. He helped feed and water the animals, clean up after the show. He was a hard worker all around, and talented."

"Cindertop?" Matt questioned. "What kind of clown name is that?"

"It was the basis of his act," replied Angela. "He was a juggling clown, and a big part of the act was juggling different objects that where set on fire. Batons, rings, handkerchiefs, flaming balls – he did it all, and was very good at it. The name came from the bit at the end of his act. He would always do a bow as the crowd cheered him on, and when he did the bow, he'd always 'accidentally' catch the top of his wig on fire. The headpiece he wore was made of a protective fire-retardant material, probably asbestos back then, so he would never really get hurt. Other clowns would come out and help to make a funny show of it as the crowd gasped. Before long, the whole tent would erupt in laughter as the clowns all worked in a comical frenzy to put out the flaming wig. I guess it was quite a riot for the times."

"So what happened?" mused Jay.

"A woman," muttered Matt. "Isn't it always?"

Jill gave Matt a sharp glare. "What is that supposed to mean?"

"All I'm saying is that once you get your heart involved in anything, things can have a tendency to get complicated,"

Matt replied. Angela looked at each of them with a sideways glance, feeling the awkwardness in the moment.

"Yes," Jill continued, breaking away her gaze as they all walked onward. It was a love triangle...or more so, a lust triangle that set the sparks flying. The Henley-Barnes Circus was owned and operated by Joseph Henley, who was also the circus ringmaster. He was known as a spellbinding master of ceremonies, a shrewd businessman, and a notorious philanderer. He gained quite a reputation in the many towns that the circus came to, often being the cause as to why the circus troupe would pack up and leave suddenly in the middle of the night."

"Lurid adventures with local wives?" quipped Jay.

"Yes," replied Lisa. "And it didn't seem to matter to him that many of these were the wives of respectable men of importance in the towns that they visited. Nor did it matter to him when he had an affair with the wife of his business partner, Edward Barnes. The story goes that Barnes found out that his wife was sleeping with another man, but he did not know that it was Henley. When Barnes came to his 'good friend and partner' with his concerns about the affair, Henley remarked that he had seen a local man about town, a man with a reputation of his own named Colin Freel, often flirting with the beautiful Mrs. Barnes. Barnes, not a small man at six-foot-four and 230 pounds, went and found the man in a local pub and beat the man within an inch of his life.

"Barnes was arrested and charged with attempted murder. He was in dire need of money for his legal defense, and Henley made him an offer – a value far less than what it was worth – to buy out Barnes' half of the circus. In desperation, Barnes agreed to the terms, only to find out later by confession of his wife that it was actually Henley that she was having the affair with. Days before his trial, Henley and the circus were gone without a trace. In a rage in his jail cell while his wife visited, he beat and strangled her into a coma before the guards could intervene. Later that night, he hung himself," Jill concluded.

The group was silent for a long moment after Jill stopped speaking. They moved on, with the only sounds being the grass and ferns being pushed aside or breaking beneath their trudging steps, and the call of crows high off in the trees, unseen against the backdrop of darkening sky as the August sun began to wane.

"Where does Cindertop come in?" asked Lisa, breaking her extended silence.

"It's part of the reason why the circus remained here in this area so much longer than many of the other places that they had set up over the years. Henley was no longer playing around with the wives of the locals. He had someone on the inside of the circus tents to fool around with. Beneath the makeup, Cindertop was handsome and articulate man, and he fell in love with and eventually married the beautiful female lion tamer who was known as Marie the Magnificent. There is no known record of Cindertop's or Marie's real names. The records of a traveling group such as theirs were often lost, mishandled or made up, often because the people were running from something in their past," said Jill.

"So, Marie, miss magnificent was banging boss man Henley," remarked Matt.

"Exactly," replied Jill. "And this went on for most of the three years that the circus remained here, right up until one night when Cindertop awoke to find his wife missing from the small cabin they lived in. It was late at night as he walked through the circus grounds. Many of the performers and assistants stayed up until the late hours and often early morning. They were, after all, mostly of a nocturnal nature. As he moved along, past many of those he saw as his close friends, he could see a strange look in their eyes."

" 'Where's Marie?' he would ask, and a friend would only turn away. 'Have you seen my Marie?' Another looked down and away, not uttering a word. Finally, one man - one of the few survivors of that night, a man named Herbert Brenton, who helped Marie care for the lions and would clean up after the elephants, offered a subtle glance toward the house that Henley had built for himself on the grounds."

"They say Cindertop tried the door, but is was locked. He walked around to Henley's bedroom window, and in the darkness of the window, illuminated by the light of several candles, he saw his beautiful Marie enrapt in the throws of passion with Henley. He stared for what seemed like an eternity before turning to see his many friends staring at him from several feet away. He soon realized that they all knew what had been going on, but no one had bothered to ever tell him. Whether they feared Henley, or just didn't care, they held their silence, and now Cindertop was made from being the top clown to just a simple fool before everyone - a fool of the heart by his friend Henley and his love Marie.

"The gathered crowd dispersed, each in their own direction, silently slithering to all of their own sleeping places. They must have decided that, whether it was guilt or shame or something else, now was a good time to cower away for the remainder of the evening. To many, it was a fatal mistake. Whatever was happening behind Cindertop's eyes in that moment was no longer human. A soulless husk of the broken man whose broken heart had hardened to a point beyond stone, and sought only to enact a vengeance upon those who had made him a bitter fool."

The group had stopped walking and stood frozen, listening to the skillful way Jill conveyed the narrative to them all. It was all of the years in her childhood being the one to tell the younger children frightening tales around late night campfires where she had found her natural skill for storytelling along with her love of dark and scary things. She quickly saw how she had them all, and couldn't hold back a slight grin as she continued.

"Having access to all of the many incendiary things that made his act unique," Jill went on, "Cindertop made his way around to the many cabins and tents that the performers and assistants made their homes. With ropes and chains, he silently secured as many of the doors as he could of the several small cabins the performers slept in, and surrounded the tents and cabins with flammable mixtures and gel-like substances that would burn hot and stick to those it came in contact with. He took the rest of his tools, props and flammable materials to the center ring of the main tent of the circus."

She stopped for a moment, looking off into the distance. She squinted her eyes for a moment. Jay shot a glance in the direction in which she was looking, but didn't see whatever it was that she may have seen.

"And what?" he asked anxiously. "What happened then?"

Jill started her forward momentum again in the direction she had just been staring. It was slow and steady as she moved on, and the others followed in behind her in anticipation of the continuation of the story.

"Cindertop broke into the house of Joseph Henley. He subdued and managed to knock out both Marie and Henley.

They awoke, tied and gagged, in chairs fastened back to back in the center of the main ring. Cindertop was in full costume and make-up, and performed an impromptu show just for them. Marie cried and pleaded through her gag for him to stop, and Henley only showed defiance and anger at the situation, not realizing the full precariousness of the circumstances. It was Herbert Brenton that discovered what was going on under the big top that night. He walked in and stood in shock as he watched Cindertop juggling his flaming batons as he danced around the helplessly bound lion tamer and her vile lover. Then, Cindertop noticed Brenton in the entranceway of the tent. He stopped his dance, smiled widely at Brenton and did his signature bow…but instead of just the top of his head lighting up, Cindertop's entire costume went up in flames."

"He didn't scream," Jill told them. "Brenton could only stand and watch as Cindertop went and embraced Marie and her lover, who were also unknowingly doused in the same flammable substance that Cindertop himself was covered in. The flames spread throughout the entire circle of the main ring, and from there quickly spread to the rest of the tent. Brenton turned and ran, listening to the screams of agony that engulfed Henley and Marie. Cindertop had set lines of flames to spread from the center ring all around the camp and grounds, and before long all of the structures were in flames. A few people got out. Many of the animals died, and a few got away. It was two weeks later that the last lion, Marie's favorite, was taken down by hunters."

"Oh…my…God," said Lisa, visibly shaken by the story. "All of this is really true? It all really happened?"

"According to witness reports, documented records, and newspaper articles, yes, it all happened…and pretty much the way Jill told it," said Angela. "I was with her when we found the story. From that, we researched where the location was of the old circus."

"So, are we close yet?" asked Matt, weary from the walk after a late night before, also trying to cover the fact that he himself was a little shaken by the story.

"We're here," answered Jill.

Matt looked skeptically at her. "How do you know?"

"There was a little folklore mixed in with the facts. It was said that in the center ring, where the fire was first started by Cindertop, something happened to the ground in the entire ring that made it so nothing ever grows there. The ground and soil produce nothing, atop a layer of charred ash and dust," Jill responded, kicking hard at the sands beneath her feet and revealing the blackened charcoal ashes that lie in a deep bed beneath the sand. "It's all right beneath our feet."

The four other people in the group looked all around where they now stood. They had not noticed, while entranced in the tale that Jill was telling, that they were all standing in a clearing in the middle of the thick woods that was nearly 30 feet in diameter and barren of vegetation, covered only in a grayish-white sand. The area was an almost perfect circle.

"It'll be dark soon," Jill said as she looked toward the edges of the circle. "Let's get things ready while we still have some light."

As the twilight passed, all the preparations were made for the nights coming event. Thirty small votive candles were placed as evenly as one can without measuring around the entire circumference of the circle. Jill knew and understood well the importance of circles when it came to acts of conjuring and communing with the dead. It was generally believed, by many of those throughout history who practiced in the arts of magic or necromancy, that a circle could contain or focus energy of a magical nature.

Jill believed that this circle in particular was bonded permanently to this place in an act of great passion and violence. All she and her friends had done was mark the boundaries of the circle with the candles to better focus the energies already within that spot. Matt and Jay lit every candle and created a smaller circle inside of the large circle with larger, brighter pillar candles on top of large stones that were more than a foot in diameter so the girls could more easily see the surface of the board as they were trying to communicate with whatever spirits might be in the area. It had been decided before they had even set out on their adventure that day that it would be best for the three girls to do the summoning, being that the guys, while intrigued by the idea, didn't have the deeply ingrained belief in what they were undertaking that evening.

Even so, Jay and Matt set up audio equipment outside of the circle to try and catch anything that happened in and around the circle. The video equipment was not night-vision capable, and with only the dim light of the candles, almost nothing would be discernable on camera, so they left the cameras in the backpack.

Matt pulled Jill's Ouija board out of his pack and carried it to the center of the circle. Angela, Jill and Lisa followed him to the place encircled by the stones and large pillar candles. They sat down on the ground, cross-legged and close enough that their knees all slightly touched. Matt set the board down on their knees and stepped away, outside of the inner circle and sat down beside Jay a few feet away.

Jay leaned in and whispered to Matt, "This is gonna be awesome, man!" While a skeptic, Jay loved the idea of doing things like this, if for nothing else than the thrill of psyching himself out for the pleasure of trying to scare himself.

"Shhhh," he whispered back to Jay as they got a sharp glare from Jill. The look from Jill didn't diminish Jay's ear to ear grin though.

The planchette – the small heart-shaped wooden plank with a perfect circle cut out in its center, stood upon tiny, felt tipped legs to slide easily around the surface of the board. Jill placed it in the center area of the board. She was the first to lay the index fingers of both of her hands on the edges of the tiny heart-shaped plank, followed by Angela, and more hesitantly finally by Lisa.

Jill began to speak.

"If there are any spirits here with us now, in our presence within or around this circle in this place, we invite you here and now to speak with us," she said, surrounded in total silence by the others in the little group.

There was nothing, not even a passing breeze or the twitch of a candle flame.

"Please, we invite you into our circle," she tried once more. "Come to us. Speak to us through our board," she went on, glancing to the other two girls, hoping something would make the planchette move.

Angela decided to try as well. "Come to us...tell us your side of the story...Cindertop..."

And with the name spoken aloud, a sudden wave of air, more direct and focused than a fleeting gust of wind, suddenly swept its way through the circle, bending the flames of many of the candles flat for a moment, but extinguishing none of them.

The planchette moved to the word –
HELLO.

Like almost all Ouija boards, it had the letters of the alphabet across the board, as well as the words 'HELLO' and 'GOOD-BYE', and the words 'YES' and 'NO'.

The girls' eyes shot up to one another, and Lisa pulled her hands away from the board.

"Lisa!" Jill exclaimed in a sharp whisper. "This is what we came here for. Don't freak out on me now!"

Lisa slowly put her fingers back on the plank.

"Cindertop...is this who is speaking to us?" Jill asked.

The plank moved to YES.

"Are you always here, trapped in this spot where you passed on?" Jill asked next.

The plank slid slightly away from the word, then returned to YES.

"Is there any way that you can move on to a better place, and be freed from this one?"

The plank moved again away from the 'Yes', and then it stopped and did not move again. The girls waited for several seconds before Jill asked another question.

"Is there something wrong?" Jill asked the spirit.

The plank moved sharply back to YES.

"What is it?" she asked.

The plank moved from letter to letter...F...A...L...S...E...F...R...I...E...N...D...S...

Jill sighed. "False friends...we know. We know you were betrayed by Marie...and by Henley..."

The plank shifted sharply and began again. N..O..T..M..Y...F...R...I...E...N...D

"I can understand Henley was not your friend..." Jill started, only to have the plank move on to one more letter before coming to a stop...S.

"Not my friends...what does he mean?" asked Lisa. "He was in love with Marie. She was more than his friend."

"And he was close with Henley. Even if Henley was just playing him, Cindertop was one of his biggest acts. Henley would have treated him like he was his best friend, even if it was all about dollar signs in his eyes," said Angela.

Jill's eyes moved back down to the board. "Help us understand. Who are the false friends?"

The plank moved slowly. Y...O...U...R...S.

Jill's eyes moved around the group. She was confused by what the board was trying to say. Matt leaned forward and watched closely what was happening inside the inner circle.

"Who?" asked Jill, with a quiver in her voice as the word left her lips.

A...N...G...E...L...A.

Angela pulled her hands from the planchette. "What is going on, Jill? What are you doing? This isn't funny!"

The planchette started to spin rapidly in a clockwise motion, startling the entire group. Jill and Lisa pulled their fingers back away from the board and sat frozen watching the small plank twirl like a ceiling fan until it suddenly stopped moving, the pointed end aimed sharply at Matt now.

Angela looked at Matt, and then back at Jill, whose eyes kept moving back and forth between her two friends.

"What...what's it talking about?" Jill muttered, with obvious confusion on her face.

Angela whipped her head toward Matt. "What is this, some kind of sick joke?" Her voice sounded of both fear and anger. "What did you tell her?!"

Matt stood slackjawed looking at the two girls. "I...I didn't say..."

Jay watched the scene from where he stood. A scent came across his nose that distracted him from what was going on in the smaller circle. Popcorn. And then other scents followed, carried from the breeze beyond the outer circle. Cotton candy…kerosene…and finally, what could possibly be the odor of elephant dung.

At the same moment, Lisa heard sounds coming from deep in the woods from all directions. First it was the music of an organ playing from the distant trees. Then she heard what sounded like laughter; the laughter of both children and adults, almost a whisper at first, and then at times louder…and closer. There was also the faint trumpeting sound like that of an elephant, echoing from somewhere deep within the dark woods. From behind her came the ominous snarl of what could be a very large cat, but when she turned to look, there was nothing but the dark.

"Do you guys smell that?" Jay asked, looking about the circle. Jill, Angela and Matt seemed oblivious to the things that were holding Lisa and Jay's attention. Lisa moved away from her three friends near the inner circle and felt a subtle panic begin to rise within her.

Angela suddenly stood up, pushing the board to the ground beside her and started to step backwards toward the outer edge of the larger circle. Jill rose to her feet and came to a place standing between Angela and Matt. There was a fury rising inside of her as the realization of what had happened came to a head. She turned her glare to Matt, then back to Angela.

"I trusted you! I brought you into our circle, and you screwed around with my boyfriend!" Jill snarled at Angela, slowly moving step by step closer in Angela's direction.

Angela stepped back, moving closer to the edge of the larger circle of candles. Tears were streaming down her face. She looked past Jill to Matt. "Why did you tell her?"

Jill spun around to face Matt. "Shut up, Matt! This is between her and I! I'll come back to you!"

As Jill's rage came forth, all of the flames of the candles surrounding the outer circle flared up more than two feet high at once, startling the entire group with the exception of Jill, who in her anger did not seem to notice. Angela began to sob harder as Jill turned her focus from Matt back to her. Jill stepped closer and closer, as Angela moved almost in sync with her further away from the others.

"I'm...*sniff*...I'm so sorry Jill...I swear, it was only one time. It was a...*sniff*...a mistake..." pleaded Angela.

"I trusted you! Both of you! And this is what you do?" Jill's face was filled with hate, her features taking an unnatural, almost animal-like expression.

"Jill, leave her alone! Please! It's not only her fault!" Matt said to Jill. Jill turned toward Matt again, and as she did, Angela came to the edge of the circle. Just as she reached it, and candles nearest to her flared again, setting ablaze her clothing, engulfing her almost in an instant.

"Jesus!" exclaimed Jay, frozen in shock at what he was witnessing, Lisa screamed while Jill, with her stare fixated on Angela, snapped out of her moment of blinding hatred and stood terrified at what was happening before her eyes. Matt ran to Angela, whose arms were flailing in all directions as she stumbled around disoriented. Matt didn't know what to do. He had nothing to throw upon her to try and smother the fire, and in his panic had forgotten about the fire extinguisher in Jay's backpack. Angela caught a glimpse of Matt in her anguish and reached out for him, grasping his arm. Almost immediately Matt was engulfed in the raging flames as well.

"Matt!" Jill wailed out, dropping to her knees. Jay lunged forward to try and help his brother, but froze once more, this time overwhelmed in paralyzing fear. Around the circle, just along the edge of the trees, Jay could make out faces, appearing as twisted images that came in and out of focus, staring at the group of teens within the circle. Some of the faces appeared to be laughing, and just below the crackling of the flames and the screams of his brother and Angela, he could hear laughter like a stifled echo deep within the dark northern woods.

Lisa could hear the laughter as well, and her whole body began to shake with fear. Jay noticed as her eyes jerked back and forth in several different directions, looking for a place to run to from the madness that was surrounding them. She took off running toward the edge of the circle, breaking through with no resistance from the candle flames. Jay called out to her to wait, but she kept running, disappearing into the darkness of the trees. He ran after her, and the faces rose up from the darkness again in the many direction he tried to go.

Finally, he pushed himself through, closing his eyes and throwing caution to the wind as he broke through the circle as well, following Lisa off into the forest. The undergrowth beneath the trees was heavier than he expected, and in the dark away from the sickening firelight of Matt and Angela's burning flesh, he soon found himself lost and tangled, feeling as if the forest trees themselves had taken hold of him, allowing him to go no further. He screamed out, but there was no help to come for him.

Jill stood in horror, tears streaming from her eyes, as she stared down at the two corpses toppled upon one another that burned before her. Matt and Angela no longer moved or writhed, and their screaming was now a miserable echo in time, one that would never leave Jill's mind for as long as she would live.

Jill looked all around her. "Lisa!" she called out. "Jay!" No one answered back. She stumbled back from the burning bodies, and noticed to her far right side that a few of the candles had flickered and died, breaking the circle of flames.

She ran. She crossed the bounds of the circle and ran another 50 feet before stopping herself. She felt something...she could feel someone watching her. She slowly turned around and looked back at the horrible scene.

The candle flames that had been out moments before were lit once more. Standing just within the boundary of the circle was a man dressed as a clown, the top of his head smoking as if it had recently been lit aflame. His head hung down, an almost sad expression was on his face.

Standing beside the clown was a small boy. The boy stood hand in hand with the clown. He looked to be less than ten years old with dark hair and wearing farm overalls. The boy looked down to the ground at first, much like the clown, but slowly he raised his eyes to look directly at Jill. The expression on his face was empty. Very slowly, he raised his right hand and waved to her, simply opening and closing his hand over and over again. Jill dropped to her knees and found herself unable to look away from the boy, unable to move...

"*They say it happened* in this very spot, about eight years ago this weekend."

Candy, the teller of the tale, looked to the four others that were with her in the little group of friends she had brought together, and waited for some response

"Bullshit," remarked Derek, the tall, thin ball player. Candy frowned.

"I heard that it happened over in Williamston, but back when my dad went to high school over there," said Bill, the high school state chess champion and brightest brain of the five. He pushed his glasses higher up on his nose, and nervously looked at the rest of the group.

"It didn't happen in Williamston," remarked Patty, the pretty red-head in the flowing summer dress. "I heard it wasn't even in this state. I think it happened out west or something."

"I'm going with Candy on this one," said Lance, the muscle bound boy with the bleached-out blonde hair. He shot a smile at Candy, who gave him the same sugar-coated smile back.

"Big surprise there," sneered Derek, rolling his eyes. Lance shot a look back at Derek. Derek ignored it.

"So," asked Bill, "what happened to Jill?"

"She was found a few days later in the same spot outside of the circle, staring at the still smoldering remains of Matt and Angela. I heard that she ended up in a mental hospital in Detroit or Cincinnati or something. A lot of people thought she murdered Matt and Angela because she found out they had an affair," Patty said.

"And what about Jay and Lisa? What happened to them?" asked Derek.

"Jay was found tangled in the brush beneath some pines about a hundred feet into the woods. He was dead, with his eyes wide open. They say he died of fright. Lisa was never found and has never been heard from again to this day," Candy told them.

"It doesn't really matter," said Patty. "We came here for a reason, and that was to have some fun and try and scare the hell out of ourselves." Patty's face lit up as she smiled at Candy. Candy walked into the small circular meadow and removed her large backpack, setting it down at her feet.

"Okay then. The sun's almost set. It'll be dark soon. Tonight, the full moon is going to rise." She reached down and unzipped her pack, and pulled out the hand-painted maple block Ouija board she found in a small resale shop a few weeks before. She held it up to the enthusiastic group of friends standing before her...

"Who wants to play?"

Rick Jurewicz

The Bond
Part I.
Lost and Found

It has been six weeks, three days and 13 hours since my older brother's body had been found half-submerged in the Strangehorn River. It was an unusually warm March day, and the river had been running fast and cold with the runoff of the rapidly melting snow.

When I say older brother, I mean that he came into the world and out of my mother 20 minutes before I did, fourteen years ago. We were identical in every way – we had the same eyes, same hair, and same teeth. It seemed like whenever we got hurt we would do it at the same time, skinning a knee or chipping a tooth.

Almost every day since his body was found, I walked down the gravel road from our house to the playground several hundred feet past the old Oak Grove cemetery. "Odd place to put a playground", Steven would say almost every time we walked there.

Steven. That is my brother's name. Mom called him Stevie, except when she was angry. We knew he was in trouble when we would hear her call out loud *"Steven James Lind!"* That was when the long, slow walk would start to the voice that called out his name. But that rarely ever happened. Steven was a good kid.

Now I walk alone to the playground. Just me: David Lind, without my big brother. There were very few other kids out and about these days, and parents were too afraid to let them out alone. The police patrolled almost all the roads, and when they saw kids out alone, they would tell them to get home now, or they picked them up and took them home themselves.

But they never talked to me. They drive by, but they don't even look at me. Maybe they can't. Maybe when they see me, they see him, and they think that they somehow failed him. It's not their fault, though. No one knew that someone was going to strangle my brother Steven and tie blocks to him and drop him into the icy river waters. No one, that is, but the person who killed him. And no one knows who that is.

At the playground there are always the same two other kids there. The blonde girl, Angela, is the same age as me. Taylor is 12, quiet and shy. At first, when Steven and I started going to that playground, Angela and Taylor always stayed on the far side of the playground away from where Steven and I played. None of the other kids from school came to that playground. Steven and I thought it was because all of the playground equipment was so old. On the underside of one of the slides, someone had scratched their initials into the bottom of the slide. It read "TJ + Alice, 1975".

It took several weeks of visiting the playground before Angela walked over to us from the far corner of the playground.

She was a pretty girl, and she always wore a clean blue dress that went down to her ankles, with a white, short-sleeve shirt that was puffy around the shoulders. There were blue ribbons tied in her shoulder-length hair, and her pale, thin lips seemed to be in a perpetual frown. She walked up to us one afternoon, probably six months before Steven had disappeared, and Steven and I froze as she approached.

"Hello," she said, stopping about 8-feet away. She was clasping her hands in front of her, nervously digging the ball of her left foot into the black sand.

"Hu...hello," Steven said. I didn't know what to say. I was used to letting Steven do all of the talking.

"That's all. Just hello. I didn't want you to think we were ignoring you," she said. She still did not smile, and just looked on between Steven and me.

"Who's your friend?" Steven asked. He nudged his head in Taylor's direction. Angela looked back over her shoulder at Taylor, who was now looking in our direction, although he quickly turned his head away when he came to realize that we were all looking at him now. Angela looked back in our direction.

"His name is Taylor. And I'm Angela. I have to go now. I'm glad we finally talked." She turned around and skipped away; she stopped skipping and sat beside Taylor when she came to him.

Steven and I said nothing to each other. We stood and stared at the two other children until Steven looked down at his watch.

"We have to get home! We are way-late for dinner!" Steven said urgently.

That was the first time we spoke to the children of the playground. There were not many times that we would visit the playground when they were not there. Sometimes they would be sitting on the old, rusted swing set, gently rocking to and fro on the plastic seats. Taylor often let his head droop sadly toward the ground. Steven and I would silently sit beside them on the open swings, and we would all swing together.

Sometimes, as Steven and I would start to swing faster and higher, Angela would join along with us. Taylor would follow Angela's lead, but he would never speak, and he would never look me or Steven in the eye. He would have the same brown corduroy trousers on, and a green and white striped long-sleeve shirt with a white collar. Steven and I thought that perhaps they were poor and couldn't afford a lot of clothes. We had never seen them in school. Steven thought maybe they were home-schooled kids, or perhaps their parents took them to another school district. Whatever the case, this place had become uniquely ours, and we came to be unique friends.

Every time I came back to the playground since Steven was found, I had kept my distance from Angela and Taylor. I didn't want to talk to anyone. When I would leave the house, I would try and talk to my mother, but all that she could do was sit at the kitchen table with a picture of Steven and drink from a bottle of Jack Daniel's whiskey and cry until she couldn't even stand up. Mom would drink and Dad would work, longer and longer hours at the saw mill my grandfather owned out on Chandler Road, east of town.

When I walked through the gates of the playground on this late afternoon, instead of heading in the direction of the merry-go-round where I spent my time slowly spinning in silence, I walked to the end of the playground where Angela and Taylor sat on the swings. I took the open swing beside Angela where Steven had often been when we came here together.

Steven liked her. He thought she was pretty. I know he did, even though he hadn't said anything to me about it. I just knew. He didn't need to say it. I thought she was pretty too, so I know Steven did. He talked to her a lot, and sometimes she would talk back, in short answers, and one time, I actually saw Angela smile at Steven, although she tried to hide it when she caught me catching her do it.

I sat beside her, and gently rocked back and forth for a short while, staring at the dusty black ground that puffed up into a small dark cloud when our feet brushed against it.

"Where is your brother?" she finally asked. I looked up from the ground and she was sitting at a dead-stop on the swing, staring directly at me. Taylor was sitting still as well, but kept his eyes fixed straight at the wrought iron fence that separated the playground from the road.

"He died", I told her.

She turned her face back to the dirt. "Oh." After a long moment had passed, she asked, "What happened to him?"

"Someone killed him," I told her. "They found his body in the Strangehorn River. He was tied down with heavy bricks, but not very well."

"Who are *they*?" she asked, looking back up at me now.

"What?"

"You said *they* found him. Who are they?"

"I...I don't know. The police, I guess."

"You weren't there? With your brother?" She asked the question, but I hadn't thought about it much before.

"No," I said. "I wasn't."

"But I thought that you were always with your brother," she said. And it was true. Steven and I were always together. All of the time. I couldn't remember any time that we weren't together.

Angela left her swing seat and stood in front of me, facing me. "David. Where were you when your brother died?"

I tried to remember. I tried so hard. My head was starting to hurt and I didn't know why. I looked up at her from the seat of my swing; she was standing right in front of me. Her face was expressionless. She almost looked sad. Almost. It was more like an empty distance in her eyes.

"I don't know…I can't remember." I let my feet to the ground and started to walk on past Angela, back toward the gate at the entrance to the playground. I didn't feel like talking anymore. It hurt to think. It hurt not to be able to remember where I was when my brother died. I should have been there with him. Why wasn't I? Where was I?

"Wait," said Angela, sharply. "Please. There is something I have to show you."

I stopped in my tracks and, with some reluctance, turned toward Angela again. At first, I saw Angela looking at me, but I shifted my eyes abruptly to what I could see far past the rear fence of the playground, far off in the thickly wooded landscape. I did not know how far it was – several hundred feet perhaps, or maybe it was several hundred yards. It was a dim and pale light, but the longer I stared at it, the brighter it became, yet still, it seemed ever farther away. I was transfixed, forgetting altogether that Angela was still staring at me.

"What do you see, David?" she asked, breaking my attention that was focused on the light in the forest.

"Do you see it?" I asked, pointing out in the direction of the light.

She turned to look, only for a moment, and then back to me. "You see a light?"

"Don't you?"

"I guess some people see things differently. Some people see different lights. Some see only shadows. I have something else to show you. Will you let me?" She held out her hand. I reached out and grasped her hand, not knowing why I was so eager to do it. Taylor left his swing seat and began to walk off toward the distant corner of the playground where so often Steven and I had seen he and Angela sitting silently.

"Where is Taylor going?"

"He doesn't like where we are going," she said.

"Where are we going?" I asked, with a slight tremble in my voice. She smiled at me, that ever-so elusive smile.

"Don't worry. You don't have anything to be afraid of."

We walked, hand in hand, to the far back area of the playground, not in the direction of the lonely corner, and not in the direction of the light, which seemed to dim the more that we moved away from its direction, although I was sure that we were closer to it than we were before.

We finally reached a small iron gate, much smaller in size than the gate at the front of the playground. There was a black iron rod that was slid down into a hollow round shaft, holding the gate closed. Angela grabbed the lever on the rod and slid it sharply upward, making a loud clanging snap when it was pushed as far up as it could go. She pulled the gate open and before us was a narrow path, almost overgrown with weeds and brush. The path went on and on, up into the dense trees of the woodlands. She started walking on down the path as I stood back, watching her move along. Something didn't feel right. I was afraid, but had no idea what I should be afraid of. Several feet ahead, Angela stopped and looked back at me.

"Come on. You need to see this. I found something you need to know," she said, her face serious and sullen. She once more reached out her hand, and I found the courage to step forward, slowly, foot over foot, to take hold of it again. We walked on for another hundred steps or more, side-by-side, until she finally came to a place where she suddenly stopped. "I think this will be far enough," she said.

"Far enough for what? Where are we?" I asked. All there was in front of us was the path, and trees of all kinds – maple, pine, oak; every kind that Steven and I had ever climbed together, as far as the eye could see.

"Turn around with me," she said. "Right now, turn with me!"

She spun herself around fast and I felt compelled to do the same, fearing some horror was waiting behind us that we'd have to fight for our very lives. But it was a different kind of horror. It was the horror that comes with an uncertainty of everything you've come to know in your life. It was the same kind of horror that came with not knowing why I wasn't there to help my brother when he needed me the most.

Behind us, and now in front of us, there was no forest to be seen. At least not the kind of thick, overgrown woodland that we had just come through to this spot where we now stood. There were enough trees to make a canopy above us, but much of the land that we had just passed across was covered with every shape and size headstone, more than I had ever seen before. How were we somehow, all of a sudden, in a sprawling cemetery? Had we walked through the woods all the way to Oak Grove? I was confused, wondering what turn we had made to come to this place. It made no sense at all.

"How did we get here?" I asked Angela, who was staring off over the vastness of the tombstones.

"We were always here," she cryptically replied.

I looked at her with what I could only imagine was a look of sheer perplexity. "Huh?" was all I could mutter, dumbfounded.

"I still have to show you what we actually came here for." She walked on, back in the direction we came, but on a slightly different path that veered to the left. I followed behind until she stopped at a small stone on the ground. It was a gravestone, standing in height only about eight inches from the ground. Angela looked down at the stone and beckoned me to stand beside her. I walked to her and stood beside her as she faced the writing on the stone.

Before I looked down, she turned her face to me and began speaking. "I didn't realize at first what was going on. The two of you were so nice. I liked your visits. But something never quite made sense to me. I didn't know until I went looking. And then I found it. I know why now."

"Why, what? What are you talking about?" I asked, shaken by the soft, cool tone in her voice.

"Why you could talk to me," she said, and pointed down to the stone in front of us.

I looked down and felt my breath leave my chest. It didn't make sense. The stone read:

DAVID MICHAEL LIND, Stillborn Infant, December 4, 2005

"What...what is this? Is this some kind of prank?" I asked, shaken even more.

"No. It's no joke, David."

"So, what? Are you telling me I died, too?" I asked her, afraid of the answer as I asked the question.

"Well. Kind of," Angela said. "Actually...you were never born."

Part II.
Reflections and Revelations

"What does that mean? I don't understand. I'm here. How can I have never been born?" I asked Angela. I was shivering now, although I wasn't cold. In fact, I'm not sure that I was feeling anything at all, except confused and a little bit frightened.

"Your headstone says that you were stillborn. I know that that means that when you were born, or would have been born, you had already died inside your mother," she said.

"But that doesn't make any sense. I have a life. I know my mom and my dad. Steven and I have friends. And Steven…we've grown up together. We've always been together…"

"Except when he died. You don't find that strange?"

"This is all strange! Nothing you are saying makes any sense," I told her. I was feeling more and more upset. I was ready to turn and run home, but I didn't know the way. We were still surrounded by cemetery as far as I could see, and I did not recognize any of it.

"David. You need to know something else. I'm a ghost, too. So is Taylor. We died, quite some time ago. That's why we are always here. We cannot go far from this cemetery, at least for very long."

"But what about the playground?" I asked. "That is where you always are. That is where we've always seen you."

"The playground isn't there anymore. It hasn't been there since the 1980s. It was old and rusted and it was torn down. The people of the town thought it was dangerous. After that, the old Oak Grove Cemetery was given the land by the town. It expanded to this place. We actually haven't walked far, only far enough to show you this," she said, pointing once again to the tombstone with my name on it. I turned from her and I thought of the many clues through my life that I would have questioned had it occurred to me to do so. Why so often Steven spoke for the both of us to people we were around. It seemed so natural. He was older, at least a little. He was the more outgoing of the two of us. I would raise my hand in class, but never get called on. I remembered how we would always share our toys at Christmas. I had thought I had wrapped packages with my name on our birthday and Christmas, but now, as I remembered, they had always only had Steven's name. How could I not know? How could I not see it?

I turned to Angela, who was still standing silently beside me as these thoughts of mine churned in my head as I came to the bleak acceptance of the truth. I asked her, "If you are a ghost too...when did you die?"

"It was in 1982," she said. She was not offering more without my prodding, although I would imagine in any circumstance how uncomfortable it might be to discuss one's own death.

"How did you die?" I asked, in little more than a whisper.

"It was an accident. The steep rocky ledges near the river, not far from the school. I slipped. My neck broke. And then I was here. I'm buried here too, like you are."

"What about Taylor?" I asked. "How did he die?"

"It was a hit and run driver," she said. "He was riding his bike on the side of the road several years ago now. He still hasn't quite gotten over it. It's why he doesn't say too much."

Then, something had occurred to me. Of all of the things that were happening, and happening all so fast, this was the one thing that I had gotten hung up on.

"You said that you died in 1982. But you look like you are still 14 years old. But you say that I was never even born, but I look just the same age as Steven did. Why is that? If I'm a ghost too, shouldn't I be the ghost of an unborn baby?" I asked.

"I…I don't know why," she said. "I have seen other ghosts before, here and there when I have walked outside of the cemetery, but they have always looked the same. Somehow, you are different. You can also stray far from your body. You're not bound to be near it. You aren't pulled back to it. You are…special."

I sat down, cross-legged, on the ground beside the stone with my name on it. Angela sat beside me and scratched her finger at the dirt in front of her. She started drawing in the sand a flower of some sort: first the center, and then carefully each petal and then finally a stem. When she pulled her finger away, the sand moved on its own as it a wind came across it and wiped the flower away.

"Where is Steven?" I asked now, looking over at Angela as she stared down where her flower had just been. "Why can't I remember what happened to him. Where was I?"

"I don't know the answers to the questions you are asking," she said. "But I do know of someone that might be able to help you."

"Who? Another ghost?" I asked.

"No, this person is alive, and she can see us. Others have talked to her. She lives in a town not far from here. I can tell you how to find her. Maybe she can help you remember, if you have forgotten. I don't know. All you can do it try. Just promise me something?"

"Okay…what is it?"

"Promise you'll come back after. Tell me what you find out."

"I will," I told her.

We walked together back toward the front gate that had once been the gate of the playground. I couldn't see the playground right now, only the rows of all of the different shaped headstones. I looked toward Taylor as Angela and I approached the gate. His eyes followed us all the way to the gate, but he did not move from his spot. I gave him a wave, and his hand rose timidly, only for a moment before falling back to his side.

I walked through the gate and thought about the next town a few miles up the road. I thought about the name that Angela had told me. Angela said that we could move in different ways as ghosts. If we concentrated on a person we wanted to see or a place that we wanted to be, we could go to that person or place with only our will. But Angela also told me that the farther away she traveled this way, she couldn't stay in that place very long at all without being pulled back to the cemetery where her body lies in the ground.

I closed my eyes and thought about the name of the person Angela told me about. I did not know where to find her, but when I opened my eyes, I saw the woman's name on the sign printed onto a steel and glass door in front of me. It read "TIFFANY REED – Psychic Counseling."

I was on a street in a downtown area. There were people walking up and down the sidewalk, eating ice cream, wearing backpacks, carrying cups of coffee and cans of soda, talking and laughing and completely oblivious to my presence. I reached out for the handle of the door now, for the first time wondering if I could even open a door, realizing that I had never done so before. The doors handle felt solid and it opened just fine as I pulled it. There was a long, narrow set of stairs that were steep and numbered 20 steps up. I quickly climbed them and came to a hall at the top of the steps that ran in both directions. A hand-painted sign pointed to the left with Tiffany's name on it, so that was the direction I took. At the end of the hall was a door painted bright yellow with flowers and ivy vines painted along its outer edge.

I stepped up and I knocked three times, and then I waited. A woman, who looked somewhat older than my mother (who was in her early 40s) opened the door and looked down at me as I stood there standing and waiting. There were dark circles beneath her eyes, but they were mostly covered with make-up, and her hair was long and brown with curls; a streak of gray hair ran the entire length of her hair down one side of her head. She smiled at me as I looked at her. My eyes were transfixed on the gaudy golden necklaces that hung around her neck. She reminded me of the gypsy fortune teller Steven and I saw at the county fair last year. Was it her? I couldn't be sure.

"Can I help you?" she asked in a friendly tone. "Are you lost?"

"No," I said, hesitantly. "I don't think so. Well, kind of. Are you someone that can help…dead people?"

Tiffany narrowed her eyes but held the friendly smile she had first greeted me with. "Well, I can communicate with the departed, yes, if that is what you mean. But that is mostly to help those left behind with unfinished business with their lost loved ones, for the most part. What is it that I can help you with? Did you lose someone?"

"Yes. My brother. He died almost seven weeks ago. Someone strangled him and put him in the Strangehorn River."

Tiffany let out a short gasp. "Come in, please, come in," she said, closing the door behind me. "I saw that on TV and I read the story in the paper. I am so, so sorry about your brother...what did you say your name was?"

"I didn't. It's David. David Lind. Steven was my brother."

"That is such a horrible thing. It's caused quite a stir around here. The police think that it was a drifter, passing through town, although I get the feeling they don't want to cause any civil unrest. Nothing civil about telling people they are safe without knowing for certain it's the truth!"

"I suppose so," I replied.

"Please, sit down. Can I get you anything?" she asked, scurrying around the room, picking things up. I recognized the bottle of Jack Daniel's she picked up from a nearby table that stood just through beaded curtains across the room. It looked as if she conducted her business in this first room, but maybe lived in the next, through the curtain.

Tiffany screwed the top of the bottle tight and I could hear her set it down clumsily on another table out of sight. She came back into the room I was sitting in and sat across a table from me, folding her hands and fidgeting nervously.

"What can I do for you now...David?" she asked, as if unsure she had heard me the first time.

"Yes. Well...I want to find my brother. I want to know what happened to him."

"I see. Well, I have to tell you, this is not an exact science. I will do my best to help you," she said. "I take it you and your brother were very close?"

"We are identical twins. We were always together. I don't know why weren't together when he died."

"Well, I would say, as tragic as losing your brother may have been, you were probably lucky you weren't with him, or you might have ended up as he did, unfortunate as that sounds. Even if you were there with him, that doesn't necessarily mean the outcome for him may have been any different, but it could have been for you."

"I am already dead, though," I said to her. A look of sadness fell upon her face.

"I know it feels like a part of you died with him. I understand. But life…life goes on, and you have to keep living for your brother…"

"That's not what I mean though…" I started to say, but she reached across the table and touched my hand. And that is when things went sideways.

Tiffany froze as if all of the muscles in her body had tightened all at once. Her jaw dropped and her eyes rolled back. Her body jolted backwards against her chair and she fell into it, and she and the chair continued to fall flat onto her back on the floor behind her. I ran around the table and leaned over her, looking down at her face as she stared back up at me in shock. I was careful not to touch her again.

She breathed deep, in and out, in and out, continuing to stare up at me.

"Are you alright?" I asked her.

"What are you?" she screamed, causing me to jump back and stumble into the wall. Tiffany scrambled to her feet and backed herself into the far wall across from me.

"I was trying to tell you," I said, feeling as startled and as scared as she was. "I am dead! Like – not alive, dead…"

Tiffany calmed herself finally, trying to get a grip on what was happening. She turned around and went through the beaded curtain, returning with the bottle she had hidden away when I first arrived. She opened it, took a long swig, and returned the cap once more to the bottle. "You are a ghost then?"

"Yes, I am. I thought you saw ghosts all the time? Isn't that what you do?" I asked.

"I talk to them," she said. "I hear them. I see them, on occasion, when they are stronger spirits, or more conflicted spirits. But I have never had one come in to my presence acting and talking like they are a living, breathing person."

"I'm sorry," I told her, hanging my head. Tiffany sighed, putting down the bottle on the floor and she stepped closer to me, but not close enough to make contact again.

"So did you die with your brother?" she asked me. "I hadn't heard that there was more than one boy killed."

"No. I didn't die with him. I mean, he was with me when I died. I died before he was born."

"I thought you said you were twins?" she asked.

"We are. I died in my mother before we were born."

Tiffany sat in silence for a very long time. She knew that this was unlike anything that she had ever come across before. This gift she had was something of an enigma at times to her, but this was a challenge she was eager to explore.

"I have something that might be able to help. Usually, I like to make direct physical contact with those that come to me for help. Physical contact initiates a deeper connection on a spiritual level. But you are different from most spirits. The energy within you is remarkable. You can travel like no other ghost I have ever seen. You are not bound to your resting place. I would also imagine that you could even, with enough concentration, make yourself visible to others like you made yourself tangible to knock on my door. But you can't remember what happened to your brother that you were always with, from even before you were born. This may require special assistance!" She held her index finger up as she said this, looking at me before springing up and out of the room.

I listened in the next room to things being shuffled around or knocked down (I couldn't be sure of which) until she came back into the room that I waited in with what appeared to be a large glass disk. She set it down on the surface of the round table in the room that I thought of as her office, and she took the seat across from where I was sitting. Once the disk was on the table, I got a better look at it. It was about a half an inch thick, and it was not clear through it like regular glass, but rather cloudy.

"This is pure crystal," she said with much enthusiasm. It was evident that all of her fears had vanished and been replaced with vigorous excitement. "Crystal, I have found, is one of the strongest conduits for spiritual energy."

"Like a crystal ball?" I asked.

"Exactly! Just like a crystal ball. But this is even better. I use this when a group of people, such as a family, all want to help contact a loved one, usually to find out if there is hidden money somewhere. No one trusts only one of them to discover any secrets that might be told from the deceased. They all want in on it, so this is what I use."

"Is there ever really any hidden money?" I asked her.

"Not usually. If there is any, it's usually not revealed to the greedy relatives that come to me."

"So, what do we do now?" I asked.

"We try and make a connection without knocking me into the wall. You place your hands on the crystal disk, and then I will, and we will try to connect on a spiritual level. What we need to do as break through your conscious mind and find what might be missing. Maybe we can find out what happened when your brother died, and maybe find out if your brother has moved on."

"Moved on? What do you mean?"

"Honey," she said sympathetically. "You're not supposed to be here. Neither is he. When you pass on, it usually means going on to a different place, not of this world. Sometimes the restless or troubled spirits get stuck here, unable to cross over. They find the light, and they go to it."

Her words made me uneasy. I never left Steven. I was always by his side. Why would he leave me behind? I needed to know more than anything what happened to my brother.

I placed my hands on the crystal. Tiffany placed her hands over the crystal as well, but she stopped for a moment. I could tell she was a little frightened at what might happen, but her hesitation ceased and her hands lowered to make full contact with the crystal disk.

I could feel something…it was like nothing I had ever felt before. A rush of sensation like I might have imagined it would be like to have electricity trickle through me veins. Not that I have veins, at least in the literal sense. I could feel Tiffany in my head as well. She was feeling the rush also. I did not know if she could see or feel exactly what I was seeing or feeling. I could see Steven, but not Steven now; it was our life together, every moment, every experience. And then, it was blackness and terror.

There was a thundering, pounding pulse deep within me. I soon realized what I was feeling was the racing heart of my brother, drowning in fear. He was scared, and he was alone. He couldn't see me. I wasn't there. But I was…Steven's overwhelming emotions blocked me away in the darkness that left his soul flailing in the shadows.

But I could see now. I could see everything. I remembered what had happened that day my brother disappeared. And I felt a powerful rage from within myself.

Tiffany's hands snapped away from the crystal disk as I opened my eyes. The palms of her hands were red from the heat that had coursed through the surface of the disk. I did not feel the heat, except in the form of the anger welling inside of me. The heated disk cracked from beneath my hand to the center of the disk.

Tiffany was breathing hard. Her eyes were wide and she was staring down at me. I could not tell if she was afraid or excited or both.

"I know what happened," I said. "I know who killed my brother."

Tiffany slowly stood up from her chair. She looked shaken. I wondered if she saw what I had seen, but I did not ask. "What will you do now?"

"I'm going to find this person. I'm going to let him know," I said to her.

"Let him know what?" she asked me.

"What it's like to be afraid," I said. I stood up from the chair and turned toward the door, and as I began to step away, she asked me one last thing.

"David? How did you know who I was? How did you come to find me?"

"A friend…she told me about the lady that could see ghosts."

"May I ask…who your friend is?"

"The blonde girl from the cemetery where I was buried. Her name is Angela. She told me how to find you, and that you could help me." I turned and opened the door that I came in through when I arrived, and then I turned to Tiffany one last time. "Thank you for your help, Tiffany. I hope it wasn't too much trouble." And then I was gone.

Tiffany stood frozen for some time after David said these final words to her. Her hands began to shake, and her eyes glassed over. It was not that she had seen what David had seen in the vision of his memory. It was something darker that clawed at her conscience from a far off place inside her mind.

Her fingers fumbled for the bottle once more that she had put aside when her enthusiasm to help the ghost boy David enveloped her. She screwed off the top of the bottle and put the mouth of the bottle near her lips; the scent of the whiskey danced up through her nostrils. Her tears streamed down her cheeks, wrecking the make-up that covered the heavy circles beneath her eyes.

She brought the bottle high up above her head with her hand and threw it down hard, smashing it into the center of the crystal disk, shattering both the bottle and the disk. She dropped to the floor, sobbing and praying. Her body was shaking. Her hands were clasped together; shards from the bottle and the crystal had embedded deep into her palms. The blood from her hand seeped through from where her hands were tightly pressed together, slowly forming a dark red line that ran down her wrist.

Her voice trembled through the sobbing that was overwhelming every fiber of her being.

"Help me, Lord. Please…I beg you…show me a way…to find absolution…"

Part III
The Killer

David stood on a lonely gravel road staring into the yard of a white two-story home. It was an older home, but well kept, and even though it was on a gravel road, the driveway of the home was cement with cracks that occasionally gave way to weeds popping through. The man who lived there was meticulous about keeping the rogue weeds in the driveway at bay.

The lawn was freshly mowed, likely done that very day. David could smell the sweet scent of the recently cut grass. He had all of the senses of a living boy, yet it occurred to him for a brief moment that he could not remember ever tasting anything before. The thought didn't linger long on his mind.

He had all of the emotions of a living boy, and the emotions that tore at him now were the sadness he felt for the loss of his brother, and the anger he felt toward the one that took him from him. He felt outside of himself, as if he was looking through the eyes of another. Now, with his memories well intact, he allowed himself to wander back to that late afternoon nearly seven weeks before. He allowed himself to feel the fear. He allowed himself the sheer horror that caused him to forget what had really happened that day so many weeks ago, but now, every terrifying detail scratched at the inside of his heart and mind...

"Why do we have to walk everywhere we go?" asked David as he kicked a stone further up the road while walking beside Steven.

"Because we just do. We always do," Steven replied, kicking the same stone as they came up to it.

"We should get bikes or something. Or maybe we should have asked Mom for a ride."

"We couldn't have asked Mom for a ride. She'd wonder why we wanted to go to Aunt Sue's. And we're going to Aunt Sue's to ask her for help to pick out a birthday present for Mom. Besides, it's finally starting to get nice out again. The snow's melting and the sun is warm. At least it felt warm when we started to walk," Steven said, rubbing his arms and regretting wearing a short sleeved shirt too early in the spring, although he did not admit it to his brother.

David felt the cold, but it didn't bother him. He was just bored from walking too long and wanted to go and visit their friends in the park. "How much farther is it?"

"I think it's only about another half mile," Steven replied.

The road was long and straight, with many large trees lining its sides; the limbs began high and reached over the road like thick fingers, giving it the feeling of a long and narrow tunnel.

The boys came upon the house with the cement driveway, and as they passed by, the man who lived there stepped out from the front door of the house. The boys looked up and saw that it was their history teacher, Mr. Mullins. He was tall, in his late 30s with light-brown hair and glasses. He looked to the boys passing on the road and gave them a quick smile and wave as he hurriedly walked over to the open hatch back of his Chevy Equinox. He pulled a large duffel bag from the hatch back before slamming it shut and headed back to the front door.

The boys waved back at him as they walked along. Once they had passed by the edge of Mr. Mullin's yard, Steven stopped.

"Why are we stopping?" David asked.

"Mr. Mullins must be getting back from another trip. He travels all around the world, and he sees cool things that he's talked about in class. I wonder where he went this spring break?"

"Steven, let's just get to Aunt Sue's. It's getting late. I want to go and see Angela and Taylor."

"I know. Maybe Aunt Sue can give us a ride to the playground after we get to her house. I want to go and see first before everybody else in class what cool stuff Mr. Mullins brought back with him."

David sighed and shrugged. "Okay, fine." They turned around and started across the large front yard, Steven leading the way. A loud noise came from the back yard that sounded like a door slamming shut. Steven looked back at David, who looked a little startled by the noise, but Steven wanted to see where the noise came from.

Steven tiptoed quietly along the side of the house beneath the windows until he could peek around the back corner into the yard. The back yard of the house was just as well-kept as the front, although there were far more trees than in the front. There was a swinging cedar-post bench beside a small man-made miniature pond that pumped water down a pile of rocks cemented together, although it only ran in the warm summer months. Mr. Mullins had several bird feeders fastened to the many trees in the yard nearest the house. With Mr. Mullins being gone on his vacation, they had been neglected and were now depleted of seed.

From the back deck of the house there was a well-worn path that led to what had most likely been the source of the noise the boys had heard – a large heavy door from what looked like a root cellar had been lifted open and then let go to slam down onto the ground beside the entrance hole. The doors were built at an angle from the ground, about 45 degrees, atop a mound of earth that looked as if it had been there for some time, well overgrown with weeds.

Steven's eyes darted around the yard looking for Mr. Mullins, but he was nowhere to be seen. David was watching just as cautiously from behind, feeling apprehensive about what they were doing.

"Steven, I think we should just go. I don't like this. We shouldn't be sneaking around, especially our teachers house. We could get in a lot of trouble!"

"Mr. Mullins is cool," said Steven. "We're not going to get into any trouble. I just wanna see what's in there."

Steven walked across the yard towards the open doorway, listening carefully all the way in case Mr. Mullins was down in the cellar. David followed behind looking around and listening as well, but neither boy could hear a whisper. When they reached the cellar door they were surprised to see how deep the cellar went. Before them was a full set of stairs that descended about 15 feet beneath the ground. There was light at the bottom of the steps that came from a dim electric bulb. Steven noticed the heavy steel lock that normally secured the thick clasp that locked the cellar door shut.

"Why do you think Mr. Mullins keeps the cellar locked with such a big lock? What does he keep down there?" asked David, not sure he really wanted the question answered.

"Let's find out," replied Steven as he stepped his first step down into the cellar.

"No, Steven! We shouldn't go in there," David pleaded.

"You don't always have to be such a scaredy-cat! I always have to talk for you and everything! Come on…please. Let's just go and take a peek."

David said nothing and followed behind Steven. The steps creaked on the way down. There was a musty smell in the air, but as they reached the bottom, the scent of vanilla filled the cold air. Shadows flickered upon the block wall in the short path ahead of them. The walls were grey and looked old, with some spots cracked from where roots from the nearby trees had broken through over the years and had been trimmed back with pruners.

Steven and David moved to the edge of where the passage turned to a sharp left and Steven allowed one eye around the corner to see if there was anyone around. He then turned the corner into a larger room and looked on with awe. David followed behind and felt the same feeling that his brother felt walking into the room, but his feeling was accompanied with a whole new sense of fear that they were in a place that they shouldn't be.

The room was roughly 10 feet wide by 15 feet deep. There was a heavy wooden table in the middle of the room, about the size of an average dining room table for four, and in the center of the table was a large white pillar candle, which was evidently the source of the flickering light they had seen on the passage wall.

The longest wall of the room caught the attention of the boys first. Fastened to the racks built into this wall, with every sort of appropriate stand for storage or display, was a vast assortment of all kinds of edged weaponry from several different cultures and historical periods. There was a samurai katana, single and double handed medieval swords and daggers, British and French cutlasses, Native American stone-carved axes, colonial hatchets and bayonette weapons from the American Civil War. There were many items the boys did not recognize, and a few that they equally found unsettling: there was a wooden baseball bat with nails driven through the thick barrel of the bat, protruding more than two inches from the opposite side, and a long shaft with three straight bayonette prongs welded to the end to form a make-shift pitchfork weapon. Both of these things looked home-made and had a particular brutality about them that outshined the other weapons in the cellar.

"Steven, we should go right now!" David said, but Steven acted as if he had not heard him. He was distracted by something else in the room.

Steven approached the far wall past the wall of weapons and took notice of the items placed on the narrow shelved built into the wall. The shelves were lined with small baby food jars. He took one of the jars from the shelf and looked at it closely, wiping a layer of dust off from the glass. Inside the jar was a gold ring with a diamond set in it. He put it back where it had been and took another from the shelf. This jar contained a silver and gold earring. He placed that one back on the shelf and walked a few feet to the left and selected another jar.

This one he stared at for almost a minute before shuddering at the realization of the contents of the jar; Steven's hand slipped, and the jar fell to the stone floor. It shattered on the impact, and the thing inside the jar, blackened and swollen, lie on the floor amid the small shards of glass.

"What...what is it, Steven? What is that on the floor?" asked David, staring at the mess.

"I think it's...I think it's a finger," he said, his voice trembling.

"Very good," said the cold voice echoing from the passage from which they had entered the room. The figure of Mr. Mullins emerged from the dark stone hall and stepped into the flickering candlelight. "If I were your biology teacher, I'd be so very impressed, especially with the object in that state of decay." Steven's eyes flashed to David, who stood frozen. Mr. Mullins looked to the place where Steven had looked, but saw nothing. "Who were you speaking to?"

"I...uh. No one," Steven uttered. He didn't know how Mr. Mullins could not see David. David remained where he was, frozen in fear and confusion. Mr. Mullins stepped to the right of the wooden table; sudden fear and instinct pushed Steven to try and run, but to no avail. No sooner had he started to move toward the passage did Mr. Mullins' quick reflexes make it easy for him to grab the barbaric looking bat from its place on the rack and throw it across the room. The top nail spike embedded into the wall just inches from Steven's face. Steven stopped suddenly and lost his footing, stumbling backwards away from the bat and falling hard to the floor behind him.

"There's no hurry," said Mr. Mullins with a smile. "I don't usually have guests here. Well, not *whole* guests. I travel so many places. It's safer that way. Mexico, China, Switzerland, London. Sometimes closer. New Orleans, Denver. I have my fun. I collect a few souvenirs along the way. At first it was something special to the person. A ring here, a necklace there. In recent years, I took it a step further," he said, nodding to the blackened thing that was once a human finger on the floor.

"You've made this very inconvenient for me, Steven. I like you. As much as I can truly like anyone," said Mr. Mullins, stepping around the corner of the table and pulling the baseball bat from the wall. He tossed the bat onto the table and took another step closer to Steven, who was still lying on the floor. Tears were coming from Steven's eyes now. He was shaking, trying to talk.

"Please…please Mister…Mist…er…Mull..llins…I won't tell anyone, I promise," Steven pleaded. David could not move and could only watch what was happening, overcome with terror. Mr. Mullins stood over top of Steven, and gently knelt beside the fear-stricken boy.

"I know you won't Steven. It's something I just can't allow," he said, almost thoughtfully, as he placed his hands around Steven Lind's neck, and he squeezed. The young boy thrashed about, using every bit of strength within him, but to no avail. The older man, his teacher; a man he looked up to and thought was 'cool', was much stronger and far too violent in nature to overcome. And David, helpless and distraught, fell deeply into himself, fading from that horrid place along with all memory of the day his brother was ripped from him…

But now, David stood at the edge of road before that wretched place once more, fully aware of the horror that happened to both himself and his brother Steven.

The darkening clouds overhead gave way to a steady rain which soon came to a full downpour. Flashes in the distant sky were followed by a low rumble, but cracked loudly after only a few minutes had passed by. The storm was coming in fast and strong.

Kent Mullins moved about in his house, grading papers, stoking the fire in the large stone fireplace, and fixing himself a fresh cup of coffee. The thunder and the rain did not phase him; he was used to turbulent and volatile things. Heavy storms actually gave him a sense of peace.

He thought about the storm in Seattle the previous summer. He had been such a gentleman to the Japanese girl visiting the family that had taken her in as an exchange student three years prior to her visit. His umbrella was extra-large and very accommodating, and he was, after all, extremely charming. She accepted his invitation to coffee, and then later still for drinks. Since that night, she has never been heard from again.

Her hair pin, though – a dragonfly encrusted with blue and green crystals – was safely enclosed in a jar in his root cellar chamber. The thought of the girl, and the hair pin, prompted Kent Mullins to glance through his back window toward the heavy wooden doors of the cellar. The lightning flashed, and Kent felt as if his heart dropped from his chest into his stomach. In that instant flash of light, he saw the two doors of the cellar wide open and the silhouette of a figure standing on the top step of the entrance to the cellar. Kent squinted his eyes and saw what looked like the figure turn toward him in the darkness before slowly turning away and descending into the cellar.

Kent's eyes searched the room around him. He hurried to the front room and looked through the pouring rain into his driveway, but saw no other vehicles except his own. He ran to his bedroom and lifted the edge of the mattress, reaching for and finding the .38 Special revolver that he kept loaded and ready.

Kent was not a fan of firearms. He preferred tools more close-quarters in nature. Knives, wires, ropes, and on occasion, when necessity called for it, his own hands. But this gun, handed down from his grandfather to his father, and then to him, was a special gift, unregistered to anyone except perhaps the killer that Kent's late grandfather took it from when he was a cop in Chicago so many long years ago. To Kent, it was an insurance policy in case something unusual were to come up and there was no time for special pleasures with sharp things.

Kent stepped out of his back door and proceeded through the rain to the open cellar. He started down the steps, edging cautiously along the cold stone wall. He quickly noticed a glow from down the passage and trained his gun in front of him. Before he could take another step, a loud crash came from above and behind him. The two doors he had just walked through were now shut, closing away the recurrent flashes from the lightning and the cold of the rain that the wind had carried down upon him. He turned and raced back up the stairs and pushed with all his might up on the heavy doors, but when they should have moved to open, they did not, as if something from the outside was holding them down.

Kent went back down the stairs and stepped slowly down the corridor, his gun up at the ready again. When he reached the corner, he peeked around and saw the figure he had seen before from his living room standing at the top of the cellar steps in the drenching rain. It was a young boy with his back now turned to Kent. The light of a candle flickered around the walls of the miserable little room. Kent stepped fully into the room with his gun aimed at the back of the boy's head.

"Hi, Mr. Mullins," the boy said without turning around. The boy's head moved slightly, not at all bothered by the presence of the man with the gun, but more so focused on the collection of the objects in the small jars on the shelves.

Mullins narrowed his eyes in the darkness, trying to discern the identity of the boy who knew his name. "Who are you? What do you want?"

David turned fully around to face Mr. Mullins. Kent Mullins gasped at the sight of the boy who he believed he had suffocated to death just weeks before. "Steven? It's not possible…"

David moved in a way that made it almost impossible for the naked eye to see, and now he was only inches from Mr. Mullins face, almost nose to nose. Mr. Mullins let out a startled scream and almost tripped stepping backwards, dropping the gun on the hard floor.

"I'm not Steven," David said coldly. "Don't you know who I am? I'm David. I'm Steven's brother."

"I...I didn't know Steven had a brother," said Mr. Mullins, with a voice that was trembling with every word.

David tilted his head slightly to the side as he continued to stare at Mr. Mullins, and then, with the same speed that he moved up close to Mr. Mullins moments before, he returned to the wall of jars, looking with great intensity upon each one. His back was turned to Mr. Mullins once more.

"You didn't know a lot of things, did you?" David spoke softly, almost seeming distracted from the fact that Mullins was still even there. "Steven has a mother and a father, too. They miss him. And these...all these people. They have people that miss them, too. They all have bonds to those who loved them in life. I can hear them, you know...faintly...there is a little piece of them in the things they left behind. That's why you take them, don't you? Because you want to keep a little piece of them."

David did not see Mr. Mullins pick the gun back up. He aimed at David's head and pulled the trigger – the shot was deafening in the small stone chamber, and left a painful lingering ringing in Mr. Mullins ears. As for the bullet itself, it passed right through David like he was nothing more than air and shattered one of the jars on the shelf. The glass shards flew around the room; a soft mist rose from the item within the jar, in this case, a small skeleton key. The mist took the shape of an old, white bearded man who was once a homeless beggar on the streets of Tulsa. The man of mist looked at Mr. Mullins and let out a wild howl as he dove right through Mr. Mullins chest from across the room, causing Mr. Mullins to grasp at his chest in deep pain.

Mr. Mullins drew in a deep breath while trying to regain his composure. He looked toward David, who now had an odd grin on his face. David stepped to the jars and held his finger beside another jar on the shelf.

"No…please, don't," uttered Mr. Mullins, seconds before David slide the jar off of the shelf and crashing to the cold floor. Another mist rose from the object that had been in the jar, a gold dollar coin that had belonged to a college freshman in San Antonio that had disappeared three years before. The young man took form in the mist, and with the same blood-curdling howl as the old man, shot through Mr. Mullins as he writhed in pain on the floor.

David had stepped away from the jars and looked down at Mr. Mullins when something else caught his eye. The wicked baseball bat with the protruding nails hung on the rack where it had been the last time David was in this room, before it had been thrown toward Steven to stop him from escaping. David walked to the rack and picked the bat from the wall of vile weapons and stepped over to Mr. Mullins, crouching low and close to his face as he lie on the floor, still trying to recover from the pain caused by the young man who'd sprung up from the mist.

"What are you going to do to me? Kill me? I don't know what you are, but if you are going to kill me, just do it already!" Mr. Mullins screamed at David.

"I'm not going to kill you. I'm not like you. I'm not like anyone. I died before I could even be born. But Steven and I…we couldn't be separated. Not by anything or anyone. Not until you. I understand that now. Our bond was so strong that nothing could keep us apart." David stood back up and walked to the wall once more. "The pain you feel…they whispered it to me…the truth is, it is the pain that you caused them in their dying moments. That is what you are feeling. That is what they are giving back to you. I wonder what would happen if you felt all of that pain at once?" David raised the bat and swung it, dragging it across the first row of jars, and then the next, and the next, until all of the jars and the trinkets of the lost souls within were strewn about the entire room.

"No no no, please…NO!" Kent Mullins pleaded to David, but the moment of no return was well passed. The mist rose quickly and filled the room. The flames from the candles flared brightly up to the ceiling of the room. In the far corner, the mist took the shape and form of the young Japanese girl with the dragonfly hair pin; she was the first of dozens of freed spirits that let forth the fiery howl, and she led the rest through the man that took each and every one of their lives. Kent Mullins screamed his own howl of shear agony as the pain of the tortured souls cut though him. The shock of it was more than any man could bear. His heart froze, and then, it burst in his chest. His eyes, ears, nose and mouth all had thick blood running from each orifice, and his body seized into a stiffened form before slumping to the cold floor one final time. There was no mist that rose from the corpse of Kent Mullins. He simply was no more.

Part IV
The Light in the Forest

Several days passed by before I decided to return to the cemetery. I could still see it as a playground when I passed through its gates, although I knew in the back of my mind what it truly was, but it strangely didn't bother me any longer.

Angela stood beside the swing set watching me as I came toward her and Taylor. She smiled as I came up to her, and I forced a smile back.

"I'm so glad you came back," she said, nervously, like she didn't believe that I would. I looked to Taylor, who, as always, sat in his sullen silence.

"Hello, Taylor," I said with a full smile.

Taylor's eyes rose from the ground into a sideways glace of his eyes. "Hi," he said to me, downtrodden and soft.

Angela looked to Taylor only for a moment before bringing her attention back to me.

"You don't have to be alone, David. You can stay here with us. We can be our own family. No one has to be alone," Angela said to me. "I've been telling Taylor that we could be."

Taylor looked up toward me once again, but he would not look at Angela. Something didn't feel right.

"I don't know if I can. Where not supposed to be here. Something isn't right. I know I told you I would come back, and I did, but I'm not sure that I'm supposed to stay here."

And then, we were no longer alone in the cemetery.

"Hello, David." A voice came from behind me. Angela had not noticed the presence of another until we all heard the voice together.

I turned around to see Tiffany standing a few yards away. She smiled at me, then looked to the others. I could tell she could see them as clearly as she could see me and I could see her. I looked to Angela, whose face looked shadowed in horror at Tiffany's presence.

"Hello, Angela," said Tiffany. The smile had vanished from Tiffany's face, and her greeting was definitely a cool one.

"What are you doing here?" Angela asked sharply. I looked on at the exchange between them and could almost feel the tension myself.

Tiffany looked back to me and stepped closer now, almost within reach. "I saw in the newspaper. The police found Kent Mullins in his cellar. An investigation has been opened into what they found in his cellar and in his home. It won't be long before they can connect a known serial killer to the disappearance of a local boy. I'm proud of you. You gave your brother some justice."

"Thanks," I said, "It was more from those that he hurt than it was me."

"But it was you that set them free. I can feel it. I know what you did for them. You've been an inspiration to me. I need to set some things straight myself in my life, starting today."

"What do you mean?" I asked. Angela quickly stepped forward toward Tiffany, who took a sudden step back.

"What are you doing, Tiffany? I think you've done enough!" barked Angela.

"What's going on? I thought you didn't know Tiffany, Angela?" I said.

"She knows me," said Tiffany. "We were in school together, many years ago. Angela was one of the popular girls. The pretty ones. Her friends did whatever she told them to do, or they would become the next subject of her public ridicule. I was the local freak. Terrible Tiffany they called me. Even back then, I could see spirits. I would see things and keep it to myself, but eventually I told one of my best friends. Lisa Danna. She wanted to be friends with the popular crowd, and told Angela about my gift. Almost immediately I became Terrible Tiffany, the freak.

"I didn't care. It was out. Either people believed me or they didn't. It didn't matter anymore. One person did believe me. Eric Vance, a boy that Angela liked…well, either liked, or just didn't like the fact that Eric didn't want her. He liked me, and one day we were supposed to meet at the ledge by the river. Eric was misled to believe that I wasn't going to be there, and instead, Angela and her friends showed up. The called me names and made fun of me, and as one point, Angela hit me in the back with a rock. The other girls thought that things had gone too far, and they all left, including Angela.

"I cried and cried, and when I finally found the strength to get up and leave, Angela came back. There was this terrible look in her eyes. She told me that Eric should be hers, and that she had had a crush on him for months. Why would he like Terrible Tiffany? She picked up another rock and hit me, but before she could do it again, I ran to her and fell on top of her. We struggled and fought, and during the fight, she came at me and went over the ledge. She fell, and when I looked over the ledge, she was at the bottom and she wasn't moving. I could feel it. I knew she was gone. I was so scared. I never told anyone what really happened."

Tears were running down Tiffany's face now. I looked to Angela, and the fierce look of hated held steady on her face. There was no remorse in her gaze, only loathing.

"Is it true, Angela?" I asked. She wouldn't speak. She just continued glaring at Tiffany as if she were anticipating something to happen. And then it came.

"I...I had a tough time after that," continued Tiffany. "I broke things off with Eric. I started drinking in high school, and I didn't ever really stop. And then I had a few too many one afternoon, many years ago, and I drove down past this cemetery..."

"DON'T you dare," hissed Angela. I could see things in Angela I had not seen before. She was emanating such hatred. She lunged toward Tiffany, but I managed to get in front of her before she could reach her and I forced Angela back. Tiffany did not budge, but there were far more tears than there had been before.

"I...I drove by and as I came closer, a girl ran into the road. But it wasn't just any girl...it was her. It was Angela...I never got over what happened with her...I'd always wished things had gone differently...and all of a sudden, there she was, and I got scared, and...I swerved..." she stopped speaking for a moment, trying to compose herself. She looked past us, at Taylor, standing beside his swing, "there was a boy, riding his bike. I hit him...oh my God, I hit the boy, and he died! There was nothing I could do...I'm so sorry, Taylor. I found out who you were, but I ran...I ran away. But I'm not running any more. I need to make things right now."

Taylor walked up to Tiffany from across the playground cemetery. She dropped to her knees, sobbing. Taylor placed his hand upon her head. Tiffany looked up at him and the little boy smiled. "It's okay...It's okay now. I know. I forgive you."

In that moment, the moment that Taylor had found a peace of his own, the spark of light in the forest had returned, growing quickly into a blinding flare. I saw it, Tiffany saw it, and Taylor saw it. Angela could see that they all were looking at something, but when she turned, she could not see the light.

Tiffany stood up and she stepped past the three of them toward what appeared to her as a blazing star cutting through the trees in the forest. "Look, David. Look at the light."

David looked and saw a figure silhouetted against the brightness of the light. He stared hard at the shape in the light until he could finally see that the figure was his brother Steven.

"That light is for you, David. It's for both of you," she said, looking to Taylor.

"No!" Angela screamed. "You said you would come back to us! You can't take Taylor away, too! I brought him here! He is mine!" She moved toward Tiffany once again, but an unseen force held her back. Tiffany took a step closer to Angela.

"You haven't come to terms with your own sins, Angela, and for that, you cannot see the light. Perhaps someday you will. Perhaps you will finally feel remorse. I am going to turn myself over to the police and tell my story. I will try to do right by Taylor, by myself, and even by you. And I pray that I never end up like you."

Angela growled out load as the force continued to pull her away, further and further. It dragged her to her stone above the ground, and as she lashed out with a final wail, it took her, deep down back into her own grave.

I stepped in the direction of the light, beginning the walk to my brother, and I noticed the boy Taylor standing behind me, afraid of what lie ahead. I walked back and reached out my hand, smiling to him, and I let him know that it was alright. He took my hand, and we walked forward, and in the next moment Steven stood before us like it was any other day, a grin from ear to ear on his face. I gave the same grin back to him, and nodded my head to Taylor.

"Steven, this is Taylor. He's coming with us today." Steven extended his hand to Taylor and Taylor reached out to him. Steven led him along into the light as I looked back behind the three of us at Tiffany.

Tiffany nodded to me with a smile, and I nodded back to her. I turned once more and continued on with my brother. My heart wasn't whole without him, and neither was his; two lonely souls, wandering and lost when we were apart. But through the thick and the thin, through the darkness and the light, through the bright summer days that we had shared or the lonely shadows of night, our bond was one that was unbreakable. And not one death, or as it was, even two, could ever be enough to keep the two of us apart.

Dark Little Corner

Way down and far beneath
In the deepest of the deep
Out of the reach of desperate light
Lying in wait beyond the night
This dark little corner of the soul
This place, this prison,
This blackened hole
While chained, this beast
Can do no harm
With claw, nor blade
Nor wicked charm,
But chains are made of many things
And fall to ruin like thrones of kings,
While the strongest bounds are forged,
From deep within the heart,
Both fear and desperation
Can tear those chains apart,
And from this cold dark place,
Set free, the beast unleashed
No longer held by bliss or joy
All lost, the hope of peace,
And from this dark little corner
That the beast did make its home,
Stares what was once the man he was,
In darkness, all alone…

Rick Jurewicz

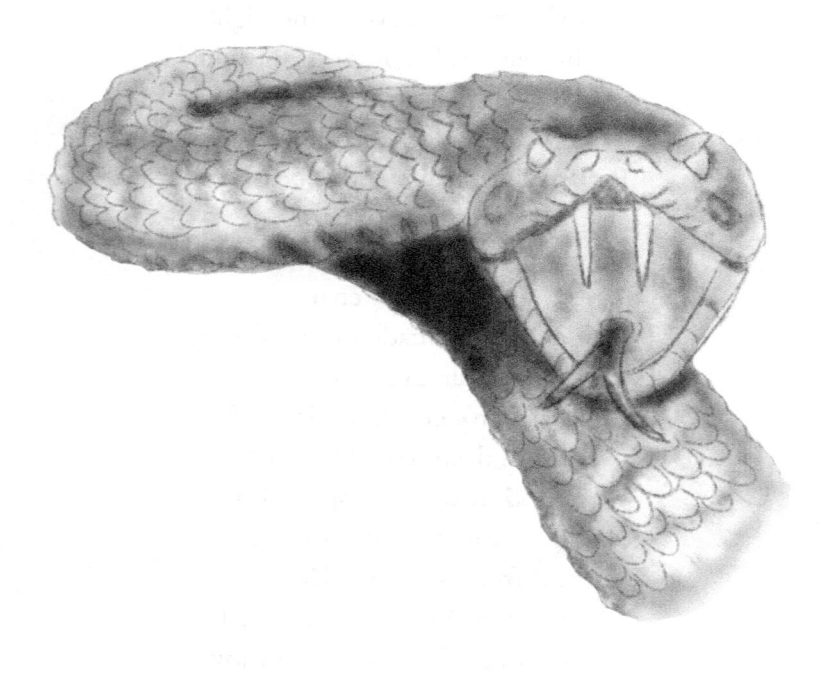

Justice

The jury was out for no longer than an hour. The charges were sparse, at best, and the jury, despite whatever their natural instincts may have told them, had little to go on.

Thomas Cobb was charged with one count of sexual assault and one count of rape. He was in his third year at Corbin-Berth University studying pre-law. He was not an extraordinarily talented or gifted student by any means, especially for a well established and accredited private university like Corbin-Berth. But where talent and gifts are lacking, money is the currency of the land. Money is *always* the currency of the land.

Judge Elway welcomed the jury back into the courtroom. Five women and seven men, all of varying age and race, marched solemnly into the room and took their seats before the court.

Sitting a few rows back behind the prosecution's bench was the victim, Theresa Kane, a bright young first-year student at Corbin-Berth who came to the university to study psychology and sociology. Sitting on either side of her were both of her parents, Marc and Jessica Kane, and in the row just behind her was her older sister by two years, Cassandra. Theresa's dream to become a children's behavioral counselor was thrown off track by the events that happened on that terrible night several months before.

It was her testimony that told the most damning tale, and in the end, it was all that the prosecution had to go on. Theresa knew Thomas Cobb from around the small campus. Thomas had the kind of personality that drew people in. Friendly, good looking and charming – a classic poster boy for the all-American man on the rise in the greatest nation in the world. But with every bright star there is a dark shadow to be cast by the demons lurking within, and Thomas Cobb had his demons.

Beyond the image of the rising star was a troubled student that never could measure up to the expectations of a demanding father that only wanted to see the family image upheld in his only offspring, and where Thomas couldn't live up to that, he felt only ridicule from Dear Old Daddy Cobb. It was only the Cobb checkbook that kept Thomas moving forward and out of the spotlight of the trail of wreckage Thomas left in the wake of his youth. DUI's disappeared. Fights that had been started and property that had been damaged by wanton reckless behavior had all but vanished with the stroke of a pen across the family checkbook.

Corbin-Berth was supposed to be a new start for Thomas. No reputation to carry along with him, and far from his old stomping grounds. Even in the age of social media and the World Wide Web, Thomas was a ghost. But his contempt for the expectations of his father and his drive to prove his own dominance - if to no one but himself - culminated in the fateful meeting on that night.

A downpour on a dark back street...

A girl alone without shelter...

A popular, friendly face driving up along side like a knight on a white horse (the horse being Thomas's white BMW M4).

Theresa testified that Thomas came out of no where that night and offered her a ride after she found herself caught in the storm. She accepted, trusting the fact that she knew who Thomas was and that he had a reputation as a decent guy that most everyone liked around campus. She admitted that she thought he was cute, but that was all. She had no interest in pursuing anything with Thomas other than a ride home in the rain.

Along the way back to her off-campus apartment, Thomas told her that he had to stop and get something from the house that he shared with three other guys. His roommates were Derek Harris, a third year theater major, Terry Frank, attending Corbin-Berth on a tennis scholarship, and Brett Greene, a pre-med student in his second year who could only afford Corbin-Berth's high tuition on a full four-year scholarship. Thomas insisted she come inside with him, suggesting it would be rude to leave her sitting alone in the car in the pouring rain.

Theresa reluctantly accepted the offer, and they went inside. The three roommates were all there, and they were all courteous and friendly, although looking back, Theresa seemed to notice a certain apprehension in their eyes.

Thomas offered her a drink, but Theresa declined. Thomas, being both charming and insistent, asked her if she would like a soda perhaps, and she accepted out of politeness and appreciation for the ride. Thomas smiled and went to the kitchen, and came back with a can of cola, open and ready to drink. At the time, Theresa didn't think anything of the fact that she was handed an open can of cola. It would only be later that that fact would have a more diabolical meaning to her.

Thomas led her to the room where he stayed, telling her that he needed to get a book that he borrowed from a professor to return it the following day. Theresa sat on the edge of a recliner in the room and sipped her soda as Thomas rummaged through a pile of books stacked neatly in the corner of the room. Theresa noticed that the rest of the room seemed to be a disorganized mess, with the exception of the pile of books that were all squarely stacked atop one another. At first, she didn't notice how tired she felt. By the time she started to feel concerned, she tried to stand up and almost fell to the floor. Had Thomas not been watching her out of the corner of his eye and caught her as she started to come down, she would have dropped straight to the floor.

As best as she could remember at that point, Thomas told her that she should lie down, and that she didn't look well. She tried to protest, but she didn't have the energy, so she laid back and noticed her vision had become fuzzy and blurred. She could remember seeing his face close to hers, and then, she faded out.

There were moments that Theresa stated on the witness stand that she could make some semblance of what was happening to her. At times, she could see him on top of her. His shirt was off, and he was moving around, back and forth. She didn't know what was happening entirely…not until after she blacked out and then came to again. She found herself face down on the bed, and he was on top of her, holding down her hands, and this time she knew what he was doing. She had little strength, and she could not fight back. She let her tears flow as he did what he did to her.

Later that night, after blacking out on the bed once more, she remembered vague visions of being taken out of a car and carried to the front porch of her apartment building. She was left lying nearly unconscious under the cover of the porch roof out of the rain. She could see through blurred vision two figures, and while she could not make them out, she remembered Thomas's voice telling the other person that they had to go right now.

When she woke up a couple of hours later, she made her way inside. She was not hurt in any way that she could tell, but she was certain that she had been raped. She told the court she felt that she needed to shower, that she felt sickly unclean, and she noticed she wasn't wearing the gold cross that she always wore that her parents had given to her for her 18th birthday. She later found it in her purse – the chain had been broken, and it had been placed in the purse at some point during the night.

Several days went by before she finally told one of her roommates what had happened that night. The roommate was Kelly Smith, another first year student that Theresa had become close with over the few months that they had been together at Corbin-Berth. Kelly insisted that Theresa go to the police, although Theresa resisted the idea at first, feeling hurt and ashamed by what had happened to her. Finally, she agreed to go in and make a report.

Statements were taken. An investigation was opened. The police and prosecution looked for any physical evidence to help support Theresa's claims, but there was none at all. Thomas's roommates were questioned, and all of them denied ever seeing Theresa there at the house the night she stated the rape had occurred. That is, at first they all denied this. Then, one story changed.

Brett Greene, pre-med, had come forward days after the three roommates were questioned and told the police a very different story, confirming that Theresa and Thomas had been there that night, and that something had went on in the room. He said he just thought they were having sex, but later saw Thomas and another person who he could not identify carrying Theresa out of the house late that night.

An arrest was made. Thomas was charged with the crime, and held on a $500,000 bond, which was quickly posted by his father. Theresa dropped out of her classes and moved home while she waited for the trial date. The entire case was based on her word and the testimony of Brett Greene. At one point during the months leading up to the trial, a mysterious gentleman that looked and sounded like a lawyer approached Marc Kane, Theresa's father, and proposed a cash offer of one-million dollars to make Theresa recant her statements and forget the whole thing ever happened. Marc told the man to go to hell and never come near his family again.

When the trial date came, Theresa gave her painstaking testimony to the court as the eyes of the local community and national media watched. She did not hide her identity. She wanted to have the face of a fighter, not a victim, although on the inside only those closest to her knew she was in a more delicate state emotionally than she had ever been in her entire life. After her testimony was over, and after she endured the cross examination of the defense team that tried to discredit her as an attention seeking harlot, the faces of the jury were all seeing the pleas of a girl in pain. Then came the testimony of the star witness, Brett Greene.

Mr. Greene entered the court room and took his spot in the witness box. And he then recanted everything that he had told the police. What the court didn't know, and was not prepared for, was that Brett was failing his pre-med classes and was going to lose his scholarship, and that a large sum of cash recently came into his possession.

Brett knew at that point he was going to Hell. This he was sure of. But at least he would get there on the Gold Line Train.

Theresa's father Marc lunged up from his seat and called Brett a liar, startling Brett in the witness stand and drawing the ilk of Judge Elway who threatened contempt of court for another such outburst. Theresa broke down in tears in her mother's arms, while Cassandra placed her hands upon Theresa's shoulders as tears welled up in her own eyes for the despair growing within her distraught sister.

After the short recess, the inevitable came to pass from a jury of Thomas Cobb's peers.

Not guilty.

The courtroom erupted in chatter and anger. But for the Kane family, amidst the outrage and tears, a solemn shadow had fallen upon them.

Cassandra was the first to leave the courtroom. She waited in the hallway for her family to come out. She was a very different individual from Theresa. While Theresa was a bright, vibrant yet slightly introverted individual, Cassandra seemed to walk a little more unconventional road. Her long, dark hair was streaked with red and purple and she wore little make-up. She her own unique fashion sense, which wasn't all too outlandish, designing her own outfits and creating clothing out of findings in resale shops and, on occasion, the hardware store. She liked to express herself in whatever way the inspiration came to her. She was a naturally pretty young woman to the eyes of almost everyone around her, but she didn't come across to others like she ever thought it of herself.

Despite what anyone's opinions of her may be based on her appearance, she proved herself to be a hard working girl that had decided a long time ago that the college life wasn't for her. She spent the first two years after high school working between 40 – 50 hours a week at a local coffee shop, eventually becoming a manager while taking an apprenticeship at a tattoo parlor. She found tattooing was a perfect outlet for utilizing her great artistic talents. That proved to be a very good move for her. She had acquired such a reputation in a short amount of time that she was able to save enough money to have her own shop and have four other very talented tattoo artists working beside her.

Cassandra was a keen study on world religions and belief systems, and had through her own research developed a very personal life practice of her own based on a combination of nature based teachings and some of the more obscure practices that, through time, misrepresentation and historical hysteria, had been cast aside as the folly of the misinformed. Many simple-minded folks would just call it witchcraft. To Cassandra, was a way of life.

Amid the growing chaos in the court room, Thomas Cobb was ushered out before most of the rest of the crowd, followed by his attorneys and his father, then the rush of reporters and onlookers. Cassandra stared at Thomas as he exited the room, and he glanced to his left and made eye contact with her. He did his best to repress a grin, but his best efforts failed him, and he let it slip, if only for a second. Cassandra only responded with the icy gaze that she held on him as he passed by, even after he looked away to attend to the crowd amassing around he and his father.

The speech made on the court steps outside of the county courthouse was a rousing tale of vindication and justice.

Justice. It spoke of the misleading lies of a money grubbing young woman who was willing to ruin an upstanding young man's future for her own gain.

Theresa and her family hurriedly walked down the steps of the courthouse as a barrage of questions and accusations came the way of Theresa and family. One reporter tried to rouse a response from Theresa by calling her out as a liar, prompting Marc Kane to lunge at the man, only at the last second being held back by the police that were escorting them from the courthouse.

The next weeks after the verdict proved to be hell for the family. Theresa's mother was laid off from her job due to the attention that had come from the trial. People close to the family wanted to believe Theresa, but they just weren't sure anymore. The reporter from the steps of the court house decided to press charges against Marc Kane for attempted assault, but privately contacted him for an exclusive with Theresa on why she made up the story in exchange for dropping the charges. Marc declined in a very abrupt manner with strong language to boot.

But then the real tragedy struck. After weeks of depression and threats made against her and her family, Theresa went out for a walk one day and didn't return by nightfall. After a short search, she was found hanging from a tree near a riverbed where she liked to play as a child. There was a note to her family apologizing for everything that had happened. She blamed herself, and just wanted this all to end. Her family and friends were crushed, but the media firestorm did not end with Theresa's death. The reporters came back in full force. The police came back to investigate her suicide.

No, the madness did not end with the life of Theresa Kane. And it certainly did not end for Cassandra.

Thomas Cobb went about his life in the months after the media circus had finally fizzled out. He had been lying low, by order of his father, and kept mostly to himself, especially after the suicide of Theresa Kane. Theresa's death had cast a shadow on him that was growing by the day. Those who initially supported him began to question the truth about what had happened the night of the suspected rape.

Brett Greene had dropped out of Corbin-Berth after being charged with making false statements to the police regarding the rape of Theresa Kane. He tried to tell the police that his reasons were jealously toward Thomas Cobb, but the reasons didn't matter to the police, or to the university Board of Educators. Brett's scholarship was revoked the second he had been charged pending the outcome of the investigation against him. Brett received probation and community service, while Thomas Cobb walked away a free man.

The money did little to ease the guilt Brett felt after Theresa's death. His life after that never amounted to anything but misery. The money was spent over the next few years on drugs and alcohol, eventually leading to his overdosing on a combination of both and falling overboard while alone on a boat he had bought with his blood money. His body was found three days later washed ashore a beach on Lake Michigan.

The trial had caused Thomas to suspend the classes he was taking for the rest of the semester. He moved out of the house he had stayed in with his former roommates and into an apartment in a small complex his father owned on the opposite side of town. He wore dark sunglasses and a hoodie when he came and went from the complex, trying to hide his identity from any onlookers who might recognize him. A certain paranoia had fallen upon him. He felt as if eyes were on him even when no one was around. At one point, he tore the apartment he was staying in apart looking for hidden cameras that he believed his father had planted to spy on him, but he found nothing.

The apartment had been left in shambles after that, so there was no way Thomas could have been able to tell that someone *had* in fact recently been in his apartment.

Cassandra Kane walked slowly and steadily down the old trail in the woods behind her grandparent's house. She would often stay at the house when her grandparents were on the road touring the countryside in their RV. The trail had been there ever since she was a little girl, and long before that. Her grandmother would take Theresa and her back on the trail when they were just little girls to pick wild blueberries, collecting bucket-loads to take back to the house and help their grandmother make delicious blueberry pies.

Cassandra could almost see in her minds eye as she walked the trail a much smaller and much younger version of Theresa and herself walking hand in hand behind Grandma, each carrying their buckets in the opposite hand. The tears started to come again, and she had to shake herself back to focus. She wiped the wetness from her eyes, smearing the small amount of mascara that lined them.

She came to the "hidden path" that the two sisters had found when they would go and play along the trail by themselves. It was a far narrower path that had been overgrown on either side by picker bushes, and they would carefully make their way through what they would call *Danger Alley* because of all of the scrapes and scratches that came with making the way through the sharp bushes. The path led to the remains of an old cement slab foundation that Grandfather had built a shed on years before. He told the girls when they were young that it was a shack where he used to boil maple syrup, but Cassandra overheard her father years later telling a friend at a poker night of the old shed back in the woods where his dad used to make moonshine. *It was only a little white lie*, she thought to herself.

The slab was secluded and private, a perfect place to have a still, she supposed, but it had served a different purpose to her in the past, as it would once again on this night.

She removed the backpack sling from her shoulder and set it upon the slab, and she sat herself down cross-legged beside the pack. The sun was going down at a steady pace, so the first things she set out around her were six pillar candles in a semi-circle in front of where she was now sitting. She lit each candle and then removed several small glass bottles from the pack and set them down around the semi-circle. In the center, directly in front of where she sat, she placed a heavy iron bowl that was about six-inches in diameter.

She opened the first bottle and poured a few drops of black liquid into the bowl. She closed the bottle and opened a second one that looked like clear, plain water, but Cassandra had taken this water from the holy water pool of a local Catholic church, and she added a single drop from the bottle to the black liquid in the bowl.

A couple of the other bottles contained various herbs that she had collected and dried from her personal garden. She crumbled each one between her fingers and dropped them into the bowl.

Cassandra took a deep breath and grasped the item that was hanging on a black cord around her neck next to Theresa's gold cross. The only thing that the cross meant to Cassandra was what it meant to her sister, but what hung from the black cord was essential to her task that evening. She removed the cord and held it up before her over the bowl. It looked like a silver bullet, but it was in fact so much more. She twisted the top and the bullet opened, and she emptied the contents into the bowl.

The grey ash that was once a part of the bones of her loving sister fell into the strange mixture in the bowl. While the candles burned bright, the bowl seemed only filled with darkness, yet Cassandra could hear a sound like sizzling as the ash came into contact with the concoction deep within.

There was one more thing to add, the final thing to commit in the invocation. The final seal. Cassandra drew from her backpack a long, sharp blade with a walnut carved handle in her right hand. She held her left hand over the bowl and drew the razors edge across her palm. She winced only a little and quickly closed her left hand in a fist. The blood gathered in her closed palm and seeped from the bottom of her fist, falling in a steady flow of drops into the bowl. As the blood fell into the mixture, she whispered a single word to herself over and over. After the fifth time she spoke the word, and without any apparent source of natural ignition, the contents of the bowl erupted into flames.

Cassandra pulled her hand away and let the contents burn down until they were a fine, black ash in the bottom of the bowl. She carefully collected the powder and placed it inside the bullet that had contained Theresa's ashes minutes before.

Cassandra extinguished each candle one by one in the order in which they had been lit, collected all of the items that she had brought with her that night, and walked back to her grandparent's house. That night, she slept the first solid sleep since the nightmare that had fallen upon her family had begun.

Thomas Cobb tired of his seclusion and decided a night out and about would not hurt anything. He still had friends out in the world, at least a few, and it was a Saturday night. He knew exactly where to find them – Club Xavier.

Club Xavier was a nightclub and popular off-campus hangout for both students and other locals surrounding the campus of Corbin-Berth. Powerful jams pulsed through the speakers around the dance floor five nights a week, with Monday and Tuesday being the only days the club closed its doors. But Saturday was the big night each week, and the house DJ was filling the dance floor with her original work as well as the house favorites.

From the moment that Thomas entered the club, something felt off. The crowd was so heavy it was hard to make his way through to the far side of the building. He didn't immediately see any familiar faces…and then, there was one. It was only a glimpse, about thirty feet and a hundred people away. It was the dark, pretty eyes that caught his attention first. The cold gaze that emanated from those eyes gripped him, and once he regained his wits he noticed the red and purple streaks in her long dark hair and realized who it was that was shooting daggers at him with those eyes.

In a flash, as strangers passed between them across the way, she was gone, yet Thomas found himself searching the masses for her as he slowly continued to move forward. He made it another six or seven feet when he saw Cassandra once again, this time in a completely different direction. She was closer now, and he felt a little shaken and disoriented, wondering how she traversed the crowd so quickly.

"Hey!" he called out to her, but much like before, she had once again vanished.

He began to move in the new direction he had seen her in. He felt a strange compulsion to try and speak to her, to try and convince her that this whole thing was a huge misunderstanding. That he was sorry about Theresa's death. Guilt wasn't a heavy burden on Thomas, but image was crucial to satisfy the demons that danced around in his head. He needed to be liked. He needed to be accepted. He needed to be *in control.*

Thomas found himself in the center of the dance floor. The pulsing music rocked his already overloaded senses and the vibrations from the speakers crept up his legs like a thousand tiny spiders overtaking his very being. He looked around him again, with a sense of dread filling his chest. And then, out of nowhere, a whisper from behind. Somehow, the sound of the music and the people dancing all around seemed to dampen as the word left her lips in no more than the whisper that it was, echoing loudly in his head.

"Justice," spoke the soft, cold voice.

Thomas turned around to see Cassandra standing behind him, her hand held up to her pursed lips. With a gentle blow, the black dust in her palm blinded his eyes and choked in his windpipe. He stumbled back, falling into those dancing around him. The dancers pushed back, thinking he was just another drunk who'd lost his bearing.

Thomas wiped at his face and opened his eyes, looking everywhere around him for Cassandra, but she was nowhere to be seen. He made his way to the rest room and washed what remained of the dust from his face, leaning over the sink and splashing water into his eyes. He cupped his hands and filled his palms with water, sipping it in and spitting the dust that remained in his mouth out into the sink. What came from his mouth looked like so much more than he had thought landed on his face, a thick paste that landed around the sink drain and slowly sunk into the dark holes down into the drain pipe.

Thomas craned his neck back as he leaned forward for another look to make sure he had washed all of the black dust from his face. In the reflection of the mirror Thomas saw standing behind him a woman in a dress, pale and sad and ever so still, staring straight into the reflection of his own eyes.

Thomas shuddered and whipped himself around, his foot slipping on a patch of water that he had accidentally splashed on the floor while washing off his face. His leg went almost straight out from underneath him, and he caught himself with his elbow on the sink as he went down, stopping him from landing flat on the floor. There was no one behind him. He eyes darted back and forth around the room, but there was nothing. There was no way someone could have moved out of his presence that fast, but it was clear that he was alone in the room.

Two men walked into the room and saw Thomas leaning on the sink, sprawled across the floor.

"You alright, buddy?" one of the men asked as he held out his hand to help Thomas up. Thomas said nothing, pulled away from the man's outreached hand in a panicked gesture, and scrambled to his feet. He pushed his way through the men and out of the restroom. He held his head down and snaked his way through the crowd and out the club door, and then made his way back to his apartment. He crawled into his bed and pulled the covers over his head, breathing heavily.

"This is bullshit," Thomas said aloud to himself. "You're letting this shit get to you. Snap the *fuck* out of it!"

He got out of his bed and made his way to the cupboard by the sink, took out a fifth of Jack Daniels and poured himself a drink. He quickly downed the first glass and poured another. He brought the glass and the bottle to the bed, where this pattern continued until both the glass and the bottle hit the floor and Thomas himself hit the bed, where he remained until the morning.

Thomas's cell phone rang early that Sunday morning. When it went off, to Thomas it sounded as if his head were inside a giant brass bell as someone beat on the bell with a hammer from the outside.

He reached the nightstand where he had left it the night before, and knocked it to the floor with the tips of his fingers as it continued to ring. He pushed himself to the edge of the bed and finally gripped the phone in between his fingers and looked at the screen. The caller ID said "Dad". Thomas sighed and ran his finger across the slide on the screen to "answer".

"Are you still in bed? You sound like shit. It's nine-thirty in the morning," said his father's voice on the other end.

"Yeah...sorry. Rough night," Thomas didn't lie.

"Do you remember I need to you to go to the family reunion on your mother's side in Vinerose Bay this afternoon?" Thomas's father asked. "Your mother and I can't make it, and showing some face time with family, getting in some pictures, it will be good for you amidst this mess that you've created."

Thomas was silent for a moment, letting out a sigh that could be heard on his father's end of the phone. His father didn't respond to it.

"Yeah...okay. I'll be there," he finally replied.

"Good," his father said, and the line went dead.

Thomas got up, showered, all the while dreading the boring drive to Vinerose Bay. At the very least the roads were paved all the way, no dirt roads to have to take the BMW down, but it was a long stretch of nothing between his apartment and the small city on the bay. Curves and hills and trees and nothing else for miles on end.

Thomas cruised along the road traveling much faster than the speed limit in his treasured car. He had only seen three cars coming from the direction of Vinerose Bay in the first fifteen minutes on the road, and then nothing for several miles after that. It was a 45 minute drive, and he passed the time listening to a rock station he found on the radio. When AC/DC's *Back in Black* came on, he turned the volume up as high as he could stand it. He was so caught up with listening to the tune and navigating the hills and curves on the road to Vinerose Bay, he did not notice at first the presence of the creature making its way from somewhere beneath his driver's seat.

The head of the jet-black snake came first, slowly working its way beside Thomas's left leg as his knee sat propped against the driver's side door. Near its neck it was almost an inch and a half in diameter. As its powerful body crept forward, it curled itself beneath the BMW's brake peddle. More of its body moved to rest in the area near the brake and the gas pedals and between Thomas's legs.

As Thomas approached a tighter curve than many he had already negotiated at higher speeds, he moved his foot from the gas pedal to the brake pedal, applying pressure to the brake...and to the body of the snake beneath the pedal. The serpent suddenly raised its head and gave a loud hiss of disapproval. Thomas gasped when he saw the snake and jerked the wheel of the car, causing it to squeal along the pavement's edge. In a near panic, Thomas pulled the wheel in the opposite direction, just enough to keep on the pavement and not end up in the deep ravine that was along that stretch of the road. He pulled his foot away from the brake pedal and moved it back to the gas pedal.

Once he had control of the car again, Thomas slowly started to lift his foot from the gas pedal…but the snake once more gave its hiss of disapproval, and Thomas pushed gently back down on the gas, maintaining his speed of nearly 66 miles per hour on one of the road's rare straight-aways. Another set of curves was coming up, and he held the car in the center of the road to try and have better luck at maneuvering the curves at the higher rate of speed. A pick-up truck came out of nowhere from the oncoming direction, forcing Thomas to swerve again to not hit the truck head on. He tried lifting his foot again from the accelerator, only to have the snake raise its head higher between his legs and hiss once more. Down went his foot on the accelerator once again.

He knew he must be getting closer to Vinerose Bay, because he was seeing more traffic, albeit sparse, on the road ahead, and he was catching up to it fast. The first car he came to he easily passed on the left hand side. The next one came as a bit of surprise to him as he only noticed it upon cresting a large straight hill. He jerked the wheel to the left suddenly, but had not anticipated the small Volkswagen Bug climbing up the other side of the hill in the oncoming lane. Thomas swerved off the road and into the gravel shoulder, kicking up dust and stones that went flying in all directions. The Volkswagen sounded its horn in angry fashion, but all Thomas could do was focus on trying to get the car back onto the pavement without losing all control and launching himself into a tumbling mess across the nearby farm field.

The tires regained their grip on the road, and Thomas found himself on the final straight shot to the town. This posed a whole new problem. He was traveling at nearly 70 miles per hour with an irritated and seemingly very large snake at his feet that bared its long fangs at him every single times he took his foot off of the gas pedal, and now it was not just the curves and hills and the occasional car to get around, but the oncoming town of Vinerose Bay itself!

His heart was racing as he saw the coming traffic light still about a quarter mile away, and sweat was coming out of every pore despite the air conditioning filing the car with cold air. He looked back down at the snake once more a couple of hundred feet away from the light…but it was not there. There was no sign of the snake whatsoever. Thomas looked back up at the coming light. It was green at that moment, and Thomas slammed on the brake pedal, gritting his teeth and, for only a moment, closing his eyes.

The tires squealed loudly as they painted thick black lines behind the locked tires as they dragged hard across the pavement surface. The car came to a complete stop. Thomas opened his eyes and breathed heavily in disbelief. His fingers were wrapped tightly around the steering wheel. He loosened his grip just a little, allowing himself a partial smile through the heavy breathing. He laughed out loud at his luck in a brief moment of relief, but in that same instant his eyes glanced up at his rear view mirror. In the reflection from the back seat he saw, once again, a pale face and sad, yet vindictive eyes staring back at him, the same eyes he had seen in the mirror of the restroom the night before. And it was in that moment that he realized what he had not noticed in seeing the face the night before. Terror overtook his senses. Thomas knew for certain now that he was staring at the face of Theresa Kane. But his moment of realization did not last long.

There was the sound first, like thunder, as if you were inside of the lightning bolt that produced the loud tear in the atmosphere that shook the world. Around the thunder the world itself was spinning out of control in a furious storm of twisted metal and razor sharp glass that was piercing and tearing flesh as the sheer force around Thomas Cobb shattered most of the bones in his body.

What was once a BMW came to rest upside down several hundred feet up the road. Thomas never even saw the large sanitation truck coming through the intersection, unable to stop at its green light before plowing into the much smaller vehicle.

Thomas hung upside-down by the seatbelt in the twisted metal carcass of a car. He could barely breathe, choking on the blood that was filling his lungs and slowly taking his life. He could not move. His spine was shattered and neck broken. All he could do, for a precious few moments longer, was see through the sweat and blood that was slowly filling his eyes.

The car had landed in front of a small grocery market. The sign above the store read *Kane Grocery*. Several people rushed to him in a desperate yet futile attempt to help him, but he looked on past them all, fixating on the glinting sunlight that shone upon an object far beyond and behind those people who tried to come to his aid. He strained to focus, and realized that it was the sunlight reflecting from a tiny golden cross that hung around the neck of a young woman who sat calmly upon the steps of the grocery store, watching the suffering man with a quiet fervor. He recognized Cassandra Kane, and in his final moments he realized the fate he had laid out for himself.

Without remorse or regret, he sowed the seeds of his own destruction. Cassandra had merely fed and nurtured what he himself had planted in the garden of fate.

As his vision went dark, beyond Cassandra's quiet gaze he once more saw, standing behind her sister, the face of

Theresa Kane. And he whispered one final word, understanding in full now its inevitable truth. With his last breath, in little more than an almost silent gasp, Thomas Cobb spoke the word…

"Justice."

Once Upon a Wicked Eve

Ol' Halloween

A goalie-masked killer is on the loose,
The hangman ties his deadly noose,
In the forest there echoes a bloodcurdling scream;
'Tis the dark splendor of ol' Halloween,

On the winds are the howls to the full silver moon,
The beasts will go stalking, and be nearer soon,
Come claw or come tooth, you're the prey in the night,
You'll find no escape in the shadows or light!

The ghouls will soon rise from the pit or the grave,
To the dead there's no difference, be coward or brave,
To haunt or to feed - man, woman or child,
There's no where to hide when the undead run wild!

The souls of the ancients crave the blood of the new,
While the cackles of witches prove your fears to be true,
And demons abound in the darkness unseen,
Oh, this is the season of ol' Halloween!

Rick Jurewicz

The Pumpkin Patch of Ernie Manville

Part I

Manville's Old-Tyme Farm was as out of the way as you could find, if you *could* find it, along the back country roads of northeastern Michigan.

Ernie Manville and his wife, Bethany, had run the farm for the past 40 years, ever since Ernie's father Bernard Manville had passed away, and Ernie's grandparents had bought the land and started the farm years before that.

It was as classic a farm setting as you could imagine; the big red barn with white accents, pens with horses and pigs and sheep, a beautiful cornfield that always produced plenty of sweet corn season after season, splendid pumpkin and gourd patches, and a small apple orchard with a dozen different kinds of apples. And people did actually find it, year after year, coming from far and wide to this unique place, traversing down the winding dirt roads from the late summertime on through the autumn harvest season.

They came in droves, the people visiting the old farm, as their parents and grandparents had years before. It was from these first families that word had spread over the years, making Manville's Farm one of the busiest out-of-the-way scenic locations in all of northern Michigan.

Ernie took great pleasure in taking tractor pulled hay wagons filled with people out to the pumpkin patch every year, five days a week through the entire month of October, to pick their own pumpkins from the twisted labyrinth of vines snaking across the ground, tromping through the rough, black and rocky dirt of the patch. Children loved to be able to go out and find their very own pumpkin, plucked straight from the earth, and have their parents haul the pumpkin back to the wagon to take back to the barn where hot cider and doughnuts awaited the whole family, courtesy of Miss Bethany.

One did not have to go out to the field to find the perfect pumpkin. The entire yard in front of the barn was filled with crates atop wooden pallets filled with bushel baskets of apples, gourds, and pumpkins. Cornstalks and pumpkins were often lined up along the outside base of the barn, around the trees and fences throughout the yard, and in front of the farm house where the Manville's lived. Weekends were always the busiest, with cars and trucks filling the often muddy parking lot and on the busiest days could be seen lined up a quarter mile down the road.

Yes, farming was a labor of love for Ernie Manville, and the fall harvest season was the big payoff of the year, not just for the produce that was sold, but the joy that came to Ernie seeing the faces of those that appreciated his hard work every autumn day.

But the last few years brought a turn that Ernie was not ready for. Bethany was a loving, hard working, sweet yet stubborn woman. She was a heavy smoker from the time before she had even met Ernie. Ernie was a smoker as well, but quit nearly 30 years before. He kept telling her that it would eventually catch up with her, but she always waved the thought away with every puff she took from a cigarette. Neither one of them was ready for it when it finally did catch up.

Bethany was diagnosed with lung cancer. The doctors told her that she had, at most, six months left, even with treatment, which she opted to not take, having seen what such treatment did to her youngest sister when she had been diagnosed with ovarian cancer years before. No, she was going to go out stubborn the way she lived, with every last natural breath she had. She did have an oxygen tank though to help get those natural breaths in the purest form that she could.

Ernie spent most of his time caring for her that year in the months after the diagnosis. He hired hands to help run the farm, depleting most of their savings. It was one cool August morning before dawn when Bethany decided that she could no longer see the suffering in Ernie's eyes. She found the strength to carry herself and her little oxygen tank to a small tool shack that was stocked with various farm tools and extra gasoline for the tractor. Ernie set it up so that if he ever ran low on fuel while far out in the field, he wouldn't have to haul it so far back to the tractor.

Bethany wasn't going to let the disease or anything else control her destiny. With the valve of the oxygen tank opened wide, Bethany lit her last cigarette.

The sound startled Ernie that morning. He looked out the bedroom window and could see, far out in the field near where the pumpkins would grow come fall, the small shack engulfed in flames. He ran downstairs to tell Bethany that the shack was on fire, that something had happened…but he didn't find her in the room where she had been sleeping the past few months. And then he knew. Stubborn woman. Stubborn, sweet love of his life…

Part II

WILSON, CRAIG and PETER, three teenage friends from Kent, the town nearest in proximity to the Manville Farm, had a penchant for looking for and finding trouble. They were not bad kids; they just made a lot of bad decisions. This day was one that they were about to make an especially bad one.

"I don't know, man," said Wilson, reacting to the idea Peter had dreamed up.

"I'm telling you," said Peter, "Cam and his parents are going out of town. I overheard him telling Luke in third period. He's pissed that they are making him go see his grandma, but she is like 95 and they don't think she will be around for much longer."

A tall and slender figure walked up from the beach away from the two girls he had been flirting with. Craig, the charmer, recently relieved of his place on the basketball team for violating student drinking rules just barely into the new season, had nothing better to do than hang out at the beach with his two best friends who helped him get into the trouble in the first place. The warmth of summer had not let go of its hold on the days well into October, but the nights still found a heavy chill in the air.

"Pete tell you what kinda crazy idea he's come up with now?" Wilson asked Craig as Craig jumped up onto a picnic table near Peter's pick-up truck.

"Yes, and I think it genius," Craig said to Wilson, who looked at Craig with the same stare that he had just had while looking at Peter.

"You too, eh?" said Wilson, shaking his head as he fiddled with a silver skull and crossbones ring that was given to him by his Uncle Bart a year before. The ring was an ongoing joke between Wilson and his uncle, who always teased Wilson since he was a little child that he was a pirate – *Captain Bart of the Good Ship "The Adventure"* - sailing the seven seas whenever he wasn't around. He brought it back for Wilson from a trip to the Bahamas and had Wilson's name engraved on the inside of the band

"Listen," Craig said with a serious tone. "Cam deals weed, we all know that. When I was on the basketball team, I overheard him talking to a couple guys that didn't know I was around the corner behind some lockers in the locker room. His parents don't know he sells the stuff, and I heard he keeps it buried under some floor boards in a shed behind their house out by the Manville Farm."

"That place where the old woman blew herself up?" asked Wilson.

"Yeah, that one," replied Craig matter-of-factly.

"So, what, we just drive up to the house and break into the shed?" Wilson asked in a half-incredulous tone. "Someone will see us and call the cops. And besides, what are we going to do with a whole bunch of weed? We start selling it to people when Cam's comes up missing, he will KILL us."

"We don't sell it," interjected Peter. "At least not around here. I have a cousin downstate that will take it all at half the street price, which will already be a lot if what I hear about how much Cam deals is true. We get quick cash, and no one knows the difference around here. Cam gets shoved into a corner for pissing off his customers, but hey, what do we care? He's a stupid-ass drug dealer."

"You're just dismissing the fact that we will be drug dealers, too," remarked Wilson.

"Minor details…Obi-Wan said it's all about your point of view," stated Peter. "If what I've heard is true, we can get nearly five-grand, and no one around here gets high from Cam's merchandise for quite a while. Call it vigilante justice…for profit!"

"You are truly a twisted individual. But still, Cam has been a major asshole as long as I can remember. Let's say I'm in – what's the plan?"

"Simple. They leave town, we park in the edge of Manville's cornfield, well off the road in the corn. We cross the pumpkin patch that runs along the edge of the cornfield, another two acres of grassy field, and through a short patch of thick woods and we will be in Cam's back yard, right near the shed. I've already scoped it out. Piece. Of. Cake."

"So how are we going to get across that pumpkin patch without being seen in the dark? I know it's way out in the middle of nowhere, but if we have flashlights and someone drives by, it's going to look suspicious…and what about old man Manville?" asked Wilson.

"Cam and his fam are leaving the night before the full moon, and the weather is supposed to be clear for days. We can make it by the light of the moon," replied Craig.

"Wait…when is the night of the full moon? Isn't that…?" Wilson paused, looking at Peter's grin and raised his eyebrows"

"Halloween," Peter uttered with a wide smirk on his face. "They are leaving the night before Halloween."

Part III

THE TWO YEARS AFTER BETHANY'S DEMISE were especially difficult for Ernie Manville. Not only was his wife and business partner gone, but most of his savings was gone as well.

He worked hard and did what he could for the crops, but his heart wasn't into it like it used to be. The help wasn't there either. He could no longer afford to pay for extra help, and he just couldn't handle at sixty-five years old what he could handle at twenty-five. As a fact of life, no man usually can.

This was the end of the line for the Manville Farm, he feared, at least under the lineage of his family. He and Bethany had no children, and he had no relatives living near the area. The fall harvest yielded less than it had in the past, but the bills kept coming in more than ever before. He no longer had the time to do the harvest hayrides. A friend and farmer from a few miles down the road, Bill Kemper, felt sorry for old Ernie and helped him out as much as he could, but Bill had to tend to his own farm and fields as well.

Still, Bill and his farm hands helped Ernie bring in most of the apples and gourds and pumpkins from the fields nearest to the barn, but they left the pumpkin patch furthest out near the cornfield alone. The pumpkins in the far field were left to grow large and wicked looking in their many different shapes and sizes, with thick twisted vines in the black soil.

Ernie found himself taking walks out to the far patch, wandering around the pumpkins and talking to them, as he often did in years before, sometimes giving certain ones names that he was especially proud of.

"You're lookin' mighty fine there today, Miss Betty," he would say, patting the large, deep orange beast of a pumpkin as he passed her by.

"Mr. Herbert, fine son-of-a-gun you are!" he spoke to another. These wonderful and wily fruits of the fall had always been a labor of love to Ernie Manville, as they were to Ernie's father, and his father before him. With all of the rest of the harvest gone, and with his sweet Bethany gone as well, this was the closest thing to love in his heart that he had left. It was bittersweet though, being so near the place where his beloved had returned, ashes to ashes literally, to the earth two years before.

He sank, and sighed, and began the long walk back to the farmhouse beside the barn. There was a late night flick on tonight, the night before Halloween. Popcorn and a movie, just like the old days with Bethany.

Part IV

THE BOYS WAITED UNTIL IT WAS GOOD AND DARK before they made their way down the country road alongside the fields by the Manville Farm.

Peter backed the pick-up truck several yards into the cornfield, with Craig and Wilson riding in the back bed. The two boys jumped out of the bed of the truck and pulled stalks of corn in front of the truck to help hide the truck in case someone were to drive by.

They started their way trekking across the field. Even bathed in the bright light of the moon, the heavily loaded and hearty vines of the pumpkin patch proved especially difficult to navigate. They tripped and fell and kicked at pumpkins in anger as they made their way through the field. Peter brought a flashlight in case they needed it in the shed, and he held onto it tightly in his hand as they cussed their way along. Beyond their occasional spitting and sputtering in anger, they continued forward in relative silence.

Ernie had fallen asleep in his chair and been there for some time. He awoke, and *Night of the Living Dead* had come on the television. He was over trying to stay up and watch, but decided it was best to turn in for the night. He turned off the TV and started toward the stairs when he noticed something through the kitchen window as he looked out toward the fields. His eyes squinted as he peered into the darkness, trying to make out what he was seeing. He saw a light out in the field…

"Pete! What the hell are you doing? Are you alright?" Craig yelled in a half-whisper, half-scream.

Peter had tripped on a vine and lost his grip on the flashlight. It hit a large pumpkin, Miss Betty to be precise, and the impact caused the light to come on and shine into the sky. The night was clear, but the heat during the days created a mist that hung low to the ground and made the beam of the flashlight look like a searchlight splitting the sky. Peter scrambled to it and quickly turned it off. He looked around at his two friends.

"Nobody saw it."

"Damn kids!" Ernie snapped, grabbing his plaid coat and knit cap. Ernie had dealt with teens from the nearby school coming into the fields over the years smashing pumpkins and wreaking havoc. Too much work, too much love went into raising his crop for any of them to be treated this way.

He grabbed a shovel and headed out the back door on foot. The light had disappeared, but that was not going to deter him from making his point and presence known if he still found anyone in his field.

The boys had made their way out of the patch, across the grassy field, and almost through the wooded area. Cam's house was just ahead, and the only light they could see was coming from the porch in front of the house. In the mist, the light from the front of the house cast strange shadows around the house, almost like what you might see in the old flying saucer alien movies from the younger days of cinema. They crept in closer, stopping just behind the shed.

Craig came around first from behind the shed and found a heavy padlock on the front double door. He pulled a crowbar from a backpack he was wearing and tried prying at the lock, but the effort was futile.

"What's the problem?" whispered Peter, stepping around from the back of the shed now, followed by Wilson.

"It won't budge!" said Craig in muffled frustration.

"Try just prying the door apart," said Wilson.

Peter snatched the crowbar from Craig's hands and forced it between the two doors and pulled hard. At first, nothing. Then, with a hard twist and push, the lock and hasp held tight and did not break, but one of the two boards from the center of the joined doors snapped loudly, breaking away from the shed door. It made a hole, but not one large enough for the boys to access the shed.

The back yard of Cam's parent's home was flooded with bright light from duel spotlights above the back door. The boys froze in fear.

"Maybe," whispered Wilson, "maybe it's on a sound or motion sensor?"

Peter started to nod his head in agreement until they saw the light come on in the house and the silhouette of a person walking toward the back door. The boys began to run.

The three of them made their way into the cover of darkness in the wooded area behind the house. The back door opened, and all they could make out was the shadow of someone stepping out into the yard and walking around. They sat still and silent, practically holding their breath as the figure surveyed the yard. Then, the figure stepped back into the house and the light went out.

"I thought you said they were going to be gone!" Craig snapped at Peter.

"I don't know who that is!" Peter snapped back. The light came back on. "Let's just get out of here!"

They began to run through the trees, using the light from the spotlights on the house to make their way through without rendering themselves unconscious from a low hanging tree limb.

"Hey! Is somebody out there?" They heard the voice carry through the thick wet air as they dodged log and limb as if it were for dear life.

Across the grassy field they strode, and then back into the pumpkin patch, jumping and sometimes tripping their way along, looking over their shoulders every few seconds in fear of being pursued.

Wilson peeked back, coming up fast near Miss Betty. Just as he turned back to face the direction in which was running, it was too late to slow himself or stop. Wilson smashed hard into Ernie Manville, holding his shovel in hand. Ernie went flying onto his back, and his head suddenly bounced as it made contact with the ground. He laid there on the dark floor of the pumpkin patch, silent and motionless.

Wilson froze, staring at the old man. "I'm sorry, I'm sorry!" he yelled aloud. The other two boys, just ahead of him, stopped and turned around when they heard him yell.

"Wilson! What's wrong?" Peter called over to him, but Wilson stood still staring down. Peter ran over to Wilson and stopped short when he saw the old farmer lying on the ground.

The moonlight reveals much in the cloudless mist of the evening hours. Ernie's eyes were wide open; the light reflected bright in the whites and in small pinpoints in his pupils. His head had struck a rock and he was bleeding badly, the blood black in the pale light. But he was still breathing.

"We have to help him!" cried Wilson, leaning down beside Ernie Manville, but afraid to touch him.

"And what? Say that we were passing by and found him here, right after a breaking and entering attempt at a nearby house? We help him, we go to jail," insisted Peter.

"But if we don't, and he dies..." started Wilson.

"Then he slipped and fell in his own pumpkin patch. It's sad, and tragic, but shit happens," said Craig. "Come on Wilson! I'm not getting arrested because you're having a soft moment. Now!" Craig grabbed Wilson by the arm and pulled him along, and Wilson gave in. They made their way to the truck and sped away.

Ernie lay unconscious, his breathing getting shallower with every breath. His final gasp came, his chest stopped moving, and he was gone. His blood soaked into the dark earth around him.

An awareness silently erupted in the moonlit spaces around him. The winds rose ever so slightly, whispering through the stalks of corn and out onto the field of pumpkins.

The ground began to shift and churn. The vines from the pumpkins began to move on their own, reaching out to Ernie's body and enveloping it with a gentle caress, clearing the dirt beneath him and pulling his body into it, returning him to its nurturing and fertile soils. And then, a lone vine wrapped itself around and through something else near the place where Ernie had laid bleeding to death in the soil...

"Shit!" exclaimed Wilson. The boys were already several miles away from the Manville Farm. "My ring...I can't find my ring!"

"So?" said Craig.

"It's got my frikkin name carved into it! I think I lost it in the field when I ran into Mr. Manville!"

Part V

The boys waited nervously throughout the next day at school, waiting to hear news that a body had been found in the Manville field. They waited for that knock on the classroom door by Principal Monroe, accompanied by several town policemen and the police chief holding a small plastic evidence bag in his hand with Wilson's skull and crossbones ring enclosed inside of it. None of these things ever came.

The final bell of the day rang and everyone headed out the door, hitting the streets for all of the Halloween fun. The younger children would gather downtown within the hour to trick-or-treat at the downtown businesses first before moving on to the side streets and subdivisions around town. A local restaurant, *The Village Italiano Deliziosoa,* closed for the afternoon and evening every Halloween to transform the entirety of their dining rooms into a haunted house for the local kids to go through for free. It cost them an evenings worth of business and a lot of hard work, but it was an exciting treat for the kids and a great time for all of the volunteers that helped to make it happen.

Peter worked at the *Village*, and he was supposed to help out that Halloween night at the restaurant with the haunting, but he and his two friends had bigger things on their minds that Hallow'd Eve.

They sat on the steps of the library a block away from the school and silently watched the children walk by in groups of goblins and superheroes and princesses and mobsters and fairies…

"We have to go back to the field," Peter finally said after several minutes of brooding.

"That's crazy," said Craig, staring at a dinosaur walking down the sidewalk in front of them. "It's stupid to go back to the scene of a crime."

"It wasn't a crime!" Wilson raised his voice. The two others looked at him sharply. He lowered his voice. "It was an *accident*, that's all. An accident."

"An accident that happened while we were committing another crime," remarked Peter. "You don't think the police are going to put together a completely different story if we decide to tell them about this *accident*? 'Yes officer, we just happened to be in that field right after someone tried to break into a shed and steal Cam's weed. What? We had to eliminate the witness that saw us trying to run away? Oh, no sir! Not us!'" Peter said mockingly.

"This is your problem," Craig barked at Wilson. "Why should we have to deal with it?"

"Because if I go down," said Wilson, "I won't even have to say anything else. The cops will put you two with me. Everyone knows we are always in everything together!"

Peter and Craig knew that Wilson was right. Craig began to fear that if any of the three of them were implicated, Cam and some of his pals would put it together that it was him that found out about the weed in the shed and come after him.

"Okay," Craig said. We go back tonight, after dark, find that ring, and get the hell out of there. Agreed?"

Peter and Wilson looked at Craig and nodded. "Agreed," they said together.

Darkness came fast that Halloween evening, with the full moon dulled in the haze of warm ground and chilled air that rose eerily across the pumpkin patch and through the cornfield of the Manville farmlands.

The boys parked the truck well off the road in the same spot as before, although a little further in than they had hidden it the night before. Each had a flashlight with them, but they agreed to only use it if it was necessary, and only in the area where they believed the ring might be. They trekked across the vines slowly; it was even more difficult in the thicker haze on this night. The moon was full, but that fact did not help them to see any more than if they had been in total darkness.

They reached the spot where they believed Ernie Manville's body had fallen, but there was no sign of the body in sight.

"I was sure this was where I had to have lost it," whispered Wilson to the others.

"Are you positive this is where you ran into him?" asked Peter.

Wilson crouched low to the ground trying to get beneath the ever thickening haze. He clicked the flashlight button on and started to look around for anything that might give him a clue that he was looking in the right place. What he hoped the most for was to quickly find the ring and get the hell out of there, but what he found sent a whole new chill through him.

"The rock," Wilson started, "This is the rock that he fell on. He hit his head right here…there is dried blood on the rock…"

"Where the hell is he?" asked Peter.

"Maybe he didn't die. Maybe he was just knocked out for a while," Craig stated, looking nervously in all directions for anyone that might be driving by on the nearby road.

"There was so much blood though," said Wilson. The wind suddenly picked up from the direction of the cornfield, pushing even thicker fog from the rows of tall cornstalks in the field.

There was a whisper in the wind, chilling and silent yet deafeningly clear:

You left him to die…

"What was that?" Peter's voice shuddered.

Craig looked around feverishly. "Is somebody out there?" he yelled.

"Craig!" Wilson yelled as low as he could at his friend. "Be quiet! What's the matter with you?"

"Didn't you hear that," Craig responded. There was obvious fear in his voice.

You all left him to die…

Again the voice floated through the winds like a poisonous snake in the grass. They all heard it; none of them could deny it or pretend they hadn't heard it.

Craig began to run in the direction that he believed the truck was in, but none of them knew what direction was what.

"Craig!" Peter yelled. "Where are you going? Craig!" He started in the direction that he thought Craig had gone. He heard a thump and a short cry in the dense fog ahead...

Craig had tripped over a large, oddly elongated pumpkin and twisted his ankle when he fell. He tried to pull himself along but stopped cold when he felt the ground beneath him starting to move. The vines slid through the wet black ground around him. He looked around in every direction, his heart was racing. The heavy vines wrapped themselves like thick ropes around his arms and his legs. The more he struggled to free himself, the tighter the vines held on. Then, they began to pull.

Peter could hear Craig struggle and then Craig began to scream, only to then have the scream muffled by a choking gasp. Peter ran in the direction he could hear the sounds coming from.

"Craig...Craig! Where are you? What's going on?" he yelled. Peter then tripped on something himself as he came to where he believed Craig's cries had been coming from.

Peter lay face down on the wet ground. He slowly pushed himself up from the mud and caught a glimpse of his hands in the moonlight, stained red. He looked around himself and found that it wasn't a vine or a pumpkin that he had tripped on. It was a leg. Just a leg, and to his left side lay an arm. And then he saw another arm...

He scrambled up from the ground and tried to scream, but no sound escaped from him. The fog had cleared in that one spot just enough to reveal a torso on the ground, and the four limbs pulled away from the torso in every direction, including the head – Craig's eyes stared wide open at the moon above, his face still holding an expression of pure terror.

Peter turned and started to run in the direction that he had come from before he found what remained of Craig.

You left him to SUFFER…

The voice tore through the night mist once more, ever so louder.

Wilson heard the voice as well, but stood frozen with fear. He could hear the footsteps pounding through the fog, but he did not know if they were Peter's or Craig's, or someone else's entirely.

Peter was running and tripping and moving in a direction that was not toward the truck or toward Wilson. Something struck him hard from behind as he ran, knocking him several feet forward onto the ground. He was stunned, and took a moment to collect himself and look back to see what had hit him.

It was a pumpkin, broken to pieces on the ground. He glared at it while he pushed himself up to his knees. Another came from his right side and smashed into the side of his head, knocking him to the ground once more. His head was throbbing with pain, but he again tried to get up, only to be pummeled by another from the opposite side, striking the left side of his head. After he lied there for several seconds, he pushed at the ground, only rising a few inches before the next one came at him, and then another, pounding down upon him.

He could see from the corner of his eye that another blow was coming, crashing down into the center of his back. He heard his spine snap, followed by a sudden scream of pain, and then he saw the pumpkin that had just come down on him rise back up above him, still attached to the long vine raised over him like a hammer. Before he could scream again, the hammer-pumpkin came down hard upon his head, leaving it looking much like the pumpkins they had kicked to pieces the night before.

Wilson stood completely still. He heard the noises and screams that had come from the field, lost in the dense fog, but now there was only cold silence.

"P-p-peter? C-c-raig? Where are you guys?" He didn't expect to hear an answer, but he got one nevertheless – one that he didn't want to receive.

P-p-Peter…C-c-raig…let him suffer…let him die…you made him die…

Wilson's legs almost let out from beneath him when he began to run. There was a light on at Cam's house, the only direction that he could make out at all, and that was where he was headed. He only made it about 100 feet before a flock of nearly 30 large black crows came out of the darkness of the night sky and flew directly at him. Several of them struck him head on as they flew, jabbing hard at his arms and torso with their sharp beaks before falling to the ground. Wilson could see in the dim light the struggling birds, scattered and broken all around him. He ducked low to the ground for cover and then started again toward the light at Cam's, but once more another menacing murder of crows bombarded him, forcing him to change his direction. He saw the cornfield ahead of him and thought that maybe he could find cover from the birds in the tall stalks of corn.

He started running to the cornfield and caught his foot on what he thought was one of the broken pumpkins on the floor of the field. His foot was lodged in something, and he shined his flashlight down on the ground. That was when he finally let out the scream that he had managed to avoid for the past several minutes.

His foot was stuck in what remained of Peter's smashed skull on the ground. It was surrounded by broken pumpkin shells. He shook it off and continued running for the corn, finally reaching the edge of the field.

Wilson slowed his pace once he entered the cornfield. Everything looked the same in every direction. The fog had subsided somewhat as he slowly made his way through the rows of corn. As he moved in the direction that he thought the truck was in, he could hear rustling through the cornstalks. Something was in the field. He pulled back from the direction of the truck and started slowly in the opposite direction, but once again, he could hear – and this time he could even see – something brush through the cornstalks and shadows. He was forced to go deeper into the field.

The thing that had lurked on either side of him was now moving at him from behind. The cornstalks rustled and swayed from different sides, but nothing could be seen to be responsible for the motion he was seeing, as if the field itself moved by a will of its own. He turned his back to the direction he was moving in, taking one steady step backwards after another so he could watch for whatever thing may be creeping toward him through the field.

As he continued to step backward, he was suddenly stopped in his tracks by something behind him blocking the way. He held his breath, afraid to look at what it might be. He felt something drop down from above him onto his left shoulder. He slowly turned his head and saw in the moonlight that it was a hand that rested upon his shoulder. On one of the fingers of that hand was the very thing - the silver skull and crossbones ring - that they had returned to the field to retrieve that night to cover their tracks.

When the realization had fully set in that a human hand, cold and still, was resting upon his shoulder, he broke free for a moment from the terror that paralyzed him and started to turn around to face the thing that was behind him. When he saw what he saw, he let out a gasp, only to have it cut short by another hand coming around from his other side. Together, the hands locked tightly around his neck. He fought with fruitless effort, pulling and clawing at the hands and arms that squeezed harder with every passing second. He looked up to see a scarecrow before him; but this scarecrow was something like he'd never before seen. The muddied hands were those of a man, with straw jutting out of the sleeves of the plaid coat that covered the upper half of its body. The legs and boots were suspended off of the ground. The body was hanging from crossed posts with its head tilting down toward Wilson as he struggled for breath.

The head was a large pumpkin carved into a jack-o-lantern, but within its shell, Wilson could see, in those final moments of his short life, the opened mouth of a man behind the shell. Dried blood had run from the corners of the mouth, and then Wilson recognized the dead-staring eyes of the man he had left dying on the rock in the field the night before; those eyes peering through the carved triangles of the jack-o-lantern's eyes. Before the final blackness came, Wilson thought he could almost see the bloodied face beneath the pumpkin shell smile at him...

A search of the town that spread to the surrounding counties would never yield any clues to the whereabouts of the three boys that had disappeared that Halloween night, nor was a body ever recovered belonging to the missing Ernie Manville. His blood was found in the pumpkin field on a large rock, as was a silver skull and crossbones ring that had belonged to one of the missing boys. A pick-up truck was found parked in the cornfield not far away, which also belonged to one of the missing boys, but no one knows how it got there or why.

What had happened that All-Hallows Eve in the fields of the old Manville Farm remains a mystery. Stories swirled and speculations were made. Was it Ernie's love for his life's work that took on a life of its own? Did something happen to stir the vengeful spirit of Ernie's departed love, Bethany Manville? The story quickly became the stuff of urban legend for countless years after the fact, drawing people from miles and miles around to the old pumpkin patch for several Halloween's thereafter.

The Manville Farm went up for tax sale, and Bill Kemper bought the land. For the first couple of years he kept the pumpkin patch going in honor of his old friend Ernie Manville - at least until it became too much of a hassle dealing with the yearly Halloween revelers. He finally just decided to let it go. But that first year after Ernie disappeared, in nearly the same place where Ernie's blood was found on a rock, Bill marveled at three huge pumpkins that grew in that very spot...and how much each of the three pumpkins *almost* appeared to have human-like faces in their twisted shells... and the most peculiar thing of all was that each of those faces ever-so-eerily resembled the faces of the three boys that went missing on that same Halloween that Ernie Manville vanished as well...

The End

One Dark Soul

A void, endless in its scope and vastness,
Teeming with bitter indifference to compassion and love,
One Dark Soul, shrouded in shadow,
Fierce in its contempt for the joys of man,
Yet staring through a mask of humanity;
Only in his smile is his true nature revealed,
Whether it be a devilish grin,
Or of soft and charming design
Do his eyes at last release in dark revelation
The dangerous creature within;
But once you've seen this smile,
Hope has passed you by;
He has you, by hook or by crook,
Leaving despair your only road left to travel;
This beast, feeding on fear,
The architect of chaotic endeavor,
Existing for the anarchic state;
He knows of no Devil, only his desire;
Whispers of a God he has heard on the breath
Of those who have crossed his path,
But no such thing has he seen;
Only fear, and tears, and rivers of blood,
Much of these in this God's name;
This One Dark Soul, faceless and ageless,
Walks on through this world for all of time,
And with his smile, lays waste to all...

Rick Jurewicz

Matchmaker

It was *agony*.

It was the only word that Lindsey could think of to describe what she put herself through every day that she sat and ate her lunch peering through the window of the Roasted Renegade Cafe and Coffeehouse on Blake Street.

Day after day she would order one of her favorite sandwich and soup combos; usually a half sandwich of some variety with avocado and a cup of one of the four piping hot homemade soup choices of the day. Today's was vegetarian vegetable with lentils. The food was always delicious. It was the mood that was tormenting.

Directly across the street from the coffeehouse was The Blake Boutique, a moderately priced yet highly fashionable clothing store where worked, as the store manager, Miss Stephanie Price. Stephanie herself was a pleasant and friendly individual to almost all who knew her, and even though Lindsey did not know her personally, she had found her to be quite the same way that most others had found her - bubbly and personable.

It was a few weeks after Lindsey realized the feelings that she was having for her coworker, Mark Tallman, that she found her way into The Blake Boutique. That was the same day that she first set foot in the Roasted Renegade. Lindsey had heard Mark talking to another coworker about going to meet his girlfriend at the boutique where she worked, as he always did for lunch. Lindsey took her lunch at the same time as Mark every day, and on that particular day decided to tail behind him.

Lindsey didn't consider herself a stalker. And what stalkers do? She just wanted to see who it was that had the heart of the man she most desperately had fallen in love with over the several months that she and Mark had worked together at Benson and Crane Marketing.

Mark was, at least in her minds eye, *perfect*. Dark brown hair, darker than her own hair, and with beaming blue eyes that popped when the blue of the clear day sky over the bay filled the office windows. He was handsome, smart, and always attentive to anyone he held a conversation with. He made everyone feel like they captured the entirety of his awareness with his piercing blue-eyed stare.

Lindsey had at first, in conversations with Mark, found his gaze unnerving. She had trouble making eye contact with him. It was his semi-crooked grin that would put her at ease. He didn't flirt with her, or any of the other girls in the office. Not really. Only enough to lighten the atmosphere in the office at times when deadlines were looming and tensions were high. But it was very clear that he was committed to the girl named Stephanie at the Boutique two blocks away.

On the day that she followed Mark to The Blake Boutique the first time, Lindsey casually slipped into the Roasted Renegade. She did not think that Mark and Stephanie would come into the cafe; Mark had stopped along the way to the boutique at an organic health food deli and picked up two paper bags carrying their respective lunches.

At first, Lindsey stood watching near the door inside the coffeehouse as Mark walked into the boutique, but it being lunch time, people started to file into the Renegade in droves, so she felt that she should buy something and find herself a seat.

She asked the server at the counter, a goth girl with the nametag "Zoey" written across it in fanciful script with black permanent marker, for just a bowl of soup. The girl Zoey did not smile when she asked Lindsey if that would be all, dispassionately passing her the empty bowl. Lindsey kept glancing towards the front window during the entire transaction. Zoey said something, although Lindsey did not hear what it was.

"I'm sorry?" asked Lindsey.

Zoey let out a sigh. "Yes. Seven-fifty."

Lindsey paid the bill as Zoey glared at her. She looked up and met Zoey's apathetic stare and felt more unsettled than she had been already. It was the first time that she had actually paid any attention to the goth girl behind the counter. Zoey's hair was long and jet black, except for a single blood-red streak that hung down in the front that had a silver skull bead tied at the end. There was a hoop piercing in the left side of her lower lip, and heavy black eyeliner around her eyes. Her lips were a dark burgundy shade, and both ears were loaded with silver spikes and hoops. She wore a Ramones t-shirt that she had cut the sleeves off of to turn it into a make-shift tank top, and had even cut the length of the shirt short revealing her barbell pierced bellybutton.

Lindsey involuntarily eyed her up and down, finally noticing the tattoos up both of her arms. Her left arm had the phases of the moon drawn up the outside of her forearm with a snake encircling the full moon in the middle. The right arm had a name tattooed up the length from the inside of the wrist to almost the inside of her elbow, in calligraphic script, that read *Adrienne*.

"Can I help you with something else?" snapped Zoey, furrowing her brow at Lindsey as Lindsey broke off her unseemly stare.

"No. Thank you." Lindsey veered away towards the soup bar quickly and did not look back at the goth girl at the counter. She got her soup - that first day it was clam chowder - and shuffled her way to the table in the window nook at the front of the coffeehouse.

Once she was seated at the round maplewood table, she finally allowed herself to look back at the girl behind the counter. Although at first she found the girl frightening, she couldn't help but feel how brave she found the girl to be. She could dress how she wanted, look how she wanted, and she could care less what others thought of it. Lindsey found a beauty in that kind of bravery. She wished that she could be more like that. Well, maybe not like *that* in particular. Just...free. She was always so conservative. No dresses above the knee. Slacks and blouses at work. No make-up. Hair pulled back in a pony tail and pale blue eyes hidden behind her dark framed glasses. *No, she was not brave*, she would often think to herself.

The girl behind the counter noticed Lindsey looking her way once more, and Lindsey quickly turned away. She did so just in time to see Mark and Stephanie walk out together and sit down at the small, round wrought iron bistro set on the sidewalk outside of the boutique. Lindsey watched them laugh and talk and touch hands, ever so gently, as they ate garden wraps and drank Bolthouse juice drinks. As she watched, she would try and imagine that it was her sitting across from Mark, touching his hand, laughing at his witty remarks, just like the ones that he would make at work.

But it was not her. It was Stephanie, who was as beautiful herself as Mark was handsome. Thin yet shapely, with hair the color of the sun on the clearest day you can imagine, long and straight. And her smile made it all the brighter. There was no doubt in Lindsey's mind how Mark had fallen in love with her.

After they were done eating, Mark gave Stephanie a quick kiss before turning to walk back up the block towards Benson and Crane. Lindsey looked at her wristwatch, realizing she only had about ten minutes left of her lunch break and hadn't even touched her soup yet. She hurriedly slurped it down, and even though it was quite cool by that point, she was aware how tasty the clam chowder was. She jumped up and rushed out the front door out onto the street in front of the Roasted Renegade.

Mark was well out of sight. Lindsey started across the street to round the corner when curiosity took hold. She stopped and looked through the front window of the Blake Boutique. She could not see Stephanie in the store front, so she decided to go on inside.

The silver racks lined the floor of the store, filled with skirts and dresses and hats and summer scarves. There was a sweet scent in the air, perfume perhaps, and Lindsey then caught sight of the counter displaying countless scents for women. There were no other customers that she could see, and at that moment, no sign of anyone else even being there until a voice startled her from behind.

"Hi. Is there anything I can help you with?"

Lindsey jumped, turning toward person behind her. She was face to face with Stephanie. Lindsey's reaction startled Stephanie as well, and she let out a cute giggle as she regained her composure.

Lindsey did not smile, and found herself in that moment without words.

"I'm so sorry," Stephanie said as her smile widened. "I didn't mean to scare you."

"I...it's alright," said Lindsey, fidgeting awkwardly with her hands, not sure what to do with them. She made brief attempts at eye contact, but found this to be quite difficult.

"Are you okay?" asked Stephanie with concern in her voice. "You seem a bit anxious. Would you like a bottle of water? I have some behind the counter." She walked around the counter and reached down into a small refrigerated cooler and brought back an ice cold bottle to Lindsey.

"Thank you," said Lindsey, removing the cap and sipping the water from the bottle.

"It's no problem, really. I used to have panic attacks. Anxiety problems. I know the look. You looked shaken. Are you going to be alright? Was there something you were looking for here?"

Lindsey was overwhelmed by just how sweet and seemingly genuine Stephanie was. She seemed to be, as first impressions go, a truly good person - yet another reason why Mark was so taken by her. Beautiful. Smart. Confident. And a huge heart. Lindsey knew she would never stand a chance.

"Thank you, no, I'm fine," Lindsey assured her as she started towards the door. "Thank you again for the water." She was out of the store and up the street before Stephanie could utter another word.

Day after day, week after week, she found herself at that table in the window of the Roasted Renegade, a voyeur into a life that was not hers, imagining what it would be like to have that life and the love of Mark Tallman. In her head she would have the conversations with Mark as if it was she herself sitting across from him. When he touched Stephanie's hand, it was her hand he was touching. When he smiled, he smiled at her.

Over time, she couldn't even see Stephanie sitting there anymore. Lindsey would eat her chicken avocado club on sourdough and enjoy her soup, and when Mark smiled at Stephanie, Lindsey would smile back as if it were a smile intended for her. Then, one day in late July, in the midst of her imaginary love affair world, Lindsey had not noticed the figure standing by her side at her regular table in the coffeehouse.

"What is it that you are doing?" the now familiar voice asked her.

Lindsey lowered her head and saw the Doc Marten boots first, and her eyes followed up the black tights that were tattered with slashes throughout to the homemade nylon miniskirt that was held together up the side with safety pins. Lindsey's eyes continued upward, past the tight fitting knit top to the face of the goth girl from behind the counter.

"Uh...what?" asked Lindsey, taken by surprise by the figure standing alongside her.

Zoey rolled her eyes and sat down uninvited in the chair next to Lindsey. Lindsey looked around, not sure of what was happening at that moment.

"I asked you what you were doing. You are here, every day. You sit here, at this table, every day. You stare out the window, smiling to yourself like a madwoman, every day," said Zoey, bluntly.

Zoey turned to look across the street and saw Stephanie and Mark. After watching them for only a few seconds, she turned back to Lindsey.

"Really?" she asked. Lindsey turned her head to the side, resting her chin on her hand. Her eyes became glassy. Zoey frowned.

"Look. I'm sorry. I know that look. I've...had that look. You shouldn't do this to yourself."

Lindsey turned to her, tears slowly running down her face, but her voice was firm.

"What do you care, anyway? What do you know about it?"

Zoey glared at Lindsey's face. Lindsey could almost feel the look like some sort of vibration or tremor. It rattled her. Zoey did not say another word when she jolted up from the chair, knocking it back against the wall behind her. She stormed away from the table and tore out of the back door of the coffeehouse. Lindsey looked on with both surprise and dismay at the goth girl's sudden departure, and it only made her feel worse.

The next day, Lindsey returned to the coffeehouse, not at her usual lunchtime self-torture session, but just after her workday had ended nearing five-thirty in the afternoon.

She stopped short of the order counter and regarded Zoey as she finished up with two teenage girls at the counter ordering caramel iced mocha lattes. Zoey gave the girls their drink pick-up tickets and looked over to see Lindsey standing by watching. Lindsey sheepishly lowered her head for a moment before coaxing the confidence out she needed to approach the counter.

"What can I help you with today, ma'am?" asked Zoey coolly.

"Listen," said Lindsey. "Can we talk? Please."

Zoey sighed and looked at the clock on the wall. The clock was made to look like an old vinyl record player, with only a minute hand and an hour hand extending from the center of the record. It was now almost a quarter to six.

"I have fifteen minutes left to my shift. You can go and wait at your usual table and I'll come see you after I clock out," responded Zoey.

Lindsey smiled. "Thank you." Zoey flashed a quick, sarcastic mock smile before Lindsey walked to the table.

After the fifteen minutes had gone by, Zoey came to the table and sat down abruptly, tossing a black leather messenger bag on the floor beside her seat.

"You weren't here at lunch today. Imaginary boyfriend on holiday?" Zoey snapped. Lindsey's head dropped for a second before she looked up at Zoey again.

"No...he actually had a business lunch meeting today," she said, almost sounding ashamed by her reply.

"So what is the deal?" asked Zoey.

"Listen, I don't want to be rude or anything. I came here to say I was sorry for yesterday. I didn't mean to talk so ugly to you," said Lindsey.

Zoey waited silently for several seconds, then said "Okay?"

"Okay...what?"

"You said you wanted to say you were sorry."

"But...I just did. Didn't I?"

Zoey gently shook her head side to side with a hint of a grin on her face. Lindsey looked puzzled.

"Okay," said Zoey. "Apology accepted." She stood up and reached down to grab her bag.

"It's just that..." Lindsey interjected, "I've never felt like this about anyone before, and I don't know what to do."

Zoey closed her eyes for a moment, released her bag back to the floor and dropped back into her chair with a thud.

"I wish," started Lindsey, "I wish I could be brave and tough like you."

"Like *me*?" questioned Zoey. "You don't even know me."

"But when I look at you, I see...*fearlessness*. You look as if you couldn't care less what anyone thinks. You seem so strong, like you wouldn't take any crap from anyone. You look like someone who is not afraid of anything!"

"Because *I look* more frightening than anything else around," said Zoey, impassively. "Look, this," she motioned to herself up and down, "didn't come about because I was fearless and full of piss and vinegar. I started dressing like this because I was afraid, of almost everyone. I didn't know how to talk to people, I didn't know how to socialize. I always felt like an outsider that everyone was talking about when I wasn't around. I'll be honest, I used to look very mousy like you back in junior high school. How old are you?"

"I'm twenty-five," said Lindsey.

"We're basically the same age," said Zoey. "I know you can remember what it was like back then, trying to fit in. I couldn't find my place, so I made my own. It was easier to get dark and weird and scare everyone else away than it was to try and fit in with a bunch of people that couldn't even figure out who they really were. They spent so much time breaking down others because they were so unhappy with who they thought they were. They were just too scared to admit it to themselves."

"At least you saw them for what they were," said Lindsey.

"Years later I did. Lindsey, you are strong for just being yourself. You don't need the guy across the street. You just need to let go and not be so afraid of things, and the right person will find you," said Zoey.

That was the first time Lindsey had heard Zoey speak her name. Her words actually sounded sympathetic and heartfelt, a sharp contrast from her normally cynical demeanor.

"I guess," replied Lindsey. She was looking down at the surface of the round maple table, unconsciously tracing the names carved into the table with her finger. 'Tracy loves Derek'. 'Tony and Maria 4-eva'. She noticed the tattooed 'Adrienne' on Zoey's arm once again.

"Who is Adrienne?" asked Lindsey, looking Zoey straight on for the first time since Zoey sat down.

Zoey turned her arm down to the table so that neither of them could see the tattoo.

"A mistake. A lesson, maybe. I don't know. Just leave it alone, okay?"

Lindsey dropped her eyes to the table once again. Zoey tapped her finger and thought, looking uncomfortable for a moment as if she was deciding whether or not to say something. Lindsey looked back up at her.

"What? What's wrong?" she asked.

Zoey bit at her bottom lip, then looked out the window across the street.

"There's...something," Zoey said, apprehensively. "You know, nevermind..."

"No," said Lindsey ardently. "What is it?"

"You are going to think I am a nut job," said Zoey. "Just let it go."

"Please," said Lindsey earnestly. "Tell me what you are thinking. I'd do almost anything..."

Zoey tilted her head and looked at Lindsey disparagingly for a moment, but she couldn't overlook the sad desperation in her eyes.

"Alright, I will tell you. But as soon as you start to think that I am crazy, just stop me and we will go our separate ways and be done with this. Deal?"

Lindsey nodded her head. "Deal."

Zoey lowered her eyes to the table in front of them, and back up to Lindsey. "Do you believe that there are things in this world that just can't be explained?"

"You mean like, how bumblebees can fly even though aerodynamically it should be impossible?" asked Lindsey.

Zoey looked blankly astonished at her before regaining her train of thought.

"No," she said bluntly, scrunching her face. It was the first time that she had looked at Lindsey like she was the freak. "I mean, like, supernatural things. Spirits, magic. The *unknown*, so to speak."

"I don't know. I've never really given it much thought," said Lindsey. "Me and a friend used a Ouija board once when we were kids. We couldn't really get it to do anything."

"A friend and I," countered Zoey.

"What?"

"It's a friend and I. Nevermind. Okay, are you at least open to the idea that the supernatural might be real?"

"I guess so. Where are you going with this?"

Zoey looked down at the table again and placed her hands flat on the surface.

"Look at this table. It's different than the other tables throughout the coffeehouse. All of the other tables were ordered together when the place opened ten years ago. They had just enough for the main dining floor. It wasn't until later that the window alcoves were remodeled to accommodate an additional table in each one. From what I was told, Sam Harris, the owner of the Renegade, is good friends with a guy that owns an antiques store the next town over. This old thing was in the basement, and the old guy told Sam he could have it if he did the refinishing himself. Sam thought it looked unique and cool, so he took it."

Lindsey never really paid much attention to the table she sat at almost every day. She focused too much on the happy couple across the way to realize that this table was different. While the other round tables through the coffeehouse looked plain with solid center spindles coming down to a flat round base, this table had a thicker wrought iron shaft that connected to an old fashioned spoked wheel rim from a 1930's Ford pick-up truck. Both the shaft and the rim were painted jet black.

"Okay. It's a nice table. What about it?" asked Lindsey.

"Look at the names carved into it. I saw you running your fingers over them before. I know who many of these people are just from working here. These two," she pointed to 'Tracy loves Derek', "I know for a fact that Derek *did not love* Tracy. In fact, he had a huge crush on Amber from the book store down the street. Every time the two of them ended up here at the same time, he stumbled over his words just trying to talk to her. But when this girl Tracy was around, he'd look right thought her, even when she couldn't take her eyes off of him."

"So what does this have to do with this fancy table?" asked Lindsey, curiously wondering where this was going.

"I'm getting to that. About a month ago, while Derek was tongue tied over Amber, I saw Tracy sitting at this table scratching something into it. After she left, I came over to clean up the table and found that she had written this with the tine of a fork. The thing is, the very next day, Tracy and Derek were in here together, all smiles, like they had been a couple for months."

"You think the table is magic or something? Like a love table?" Lindsey said, her tone beyond mere skepticism.

"No. I am certain it is. I knew you'd think I was crazy. I've...I've seen this table work. All of these people I've seen together here and other places whereas before their names were on the table they had almost nothing to do with each other. I don't know how, I don't know why. It's the real deal," said Zoey.

Lindsey was speechless. Yet, she found herself not able to completely disregard Zoey's tale of the table, and she didn't know why. Zoey was right. It did sound crazy. But what if it was true?

"I gotta go," said Zoey suddenly, rising from her chair. "I have laundry to do, and they are having me open tomorrow morning. I hate the breakfast shift. Are you gonna be alright?"

"Yeah. I'm ok. Thanks for listening to me. And thanks for letting me apologize," said Lindsey as she got up from her chair to leave as well.

"I know it's pretty fantastical, what I told you about the table. To be honest, I don't think you should do it. I don't think you need it. Maybe this guy just isn't the one," Zoey suggested.

Lindsey pressed her lips together firmly, giving Zoey a nod that said to Zoey 'I hear what you are saying but I just can't accept that right now'.

"But if you do try it," warned Zoey, "Don't carve the names too deeply into the wood. All it should take is just deep enough to make a connection, to reveal something that wasn't seen before. The rest may come naturally. But the deeper the name is carved, the deeper the desire. Don't let yourself be fooled. Desire too deep can be a dangerous thing."

 Several days had passed after the conversation with Zoey, and Lindsey had not returned to the Roasted Renegade. She was trying to do everything within her willpower to ignore the feelings she had for Mark. That also meant staying away from the coffeehouse on her lunch breaks.
 She found herself walking up the street that Benson and Crane was on during her lunches to a small hole-in-the-wall pub that had fantastic burgers and French dip sandwiches. She was missing her avocado and sourdough favorites with the soup du jour, but she was saving herself from the self-inflicted pain of watching the man she loved enthralled daily with a perfect woman, the woman that he loved instead of her.
 A whole week went by, and everyone in the office had been wrapped up in the hotel project that had a deadline that came to term in three days. The project was almost completed; Mark had lead on the team working on the presentation. He had at several times during the last two weeks came and asked Lindsey's thoughts on many of his ideas, and quite often used her input to make changes. It was yet another thing that she loved about him - he recognized her contributions to the company and the team in ways that others did not.
 Now it was early Friday morning, and the final details were being worked out. Mark came in with an exceptionally bright smile that morning. Lindsey watched as he walked from the main entry door and approached Kyle Zeffer, another member of Mark's main team and a close friend of Mark's.
 The exchange seemed casual at first. Nods and smiles, until suddenly Kyle's face lit up with a brief, hearty laugh. Kyle

patted Mark on the shoulder and the two men exchanged a quick hug, which attracted the attention of others in the office.

Lindsey's eyes widened and the color had left her face as she saw others in the office coming up to the two men, smiles growing on everyone's faces as they circled around Mark. She got up as well, and cautiously moved nearer to the crowd. Mark looked over and saw Lindsey coming.

"Lindsey! What do you think?" Mark asked excitedly. He lunged out with his left hand a small, white padded box with the largest diamond that she had ever laid her eyes on. "I'm proposing to Steph today. We meet every day at her work for lunch. I thought it would be perfect to do it there!"

Lindsey couldn't find any air in her lungs at first to form words. Initially she just forced a false smile to her face. She looked up from the diamond and felt desperate to say something to make the moment less uncomfortable.

"That...that is beautiful, Mark," she forced out, holding back tears. The other men around were still coming up and giving him pats on the back, while the female coworkers were giving him hugs and ogling the brilliant diamond engagement ring. Lindsey used the cloud of chaos in the office to slip away and out of the building.

She walked hurriedly around the backside of the building and stepped into a narrow alleyway. She could not hold back the tears any longer. Lindsey's knees gave way as she slid backwards down the white brick wall, deeply sobbing.

After several minutes went by, Lindsey composed herself as much as she possibly could, and forced herself back to her feet. She knew that she couldn't possibly return to the office that day. She dialed her cell phone to call Liz at the main office desk, telling her that she suddenly did not feel so well and had to leave the office. Liz took note of it and told her that she hoped she feels better soon. Lindsey did not think that that was likely.

Lindsey walked around the block and down a side street. After a left and then another left, she found herself rounding Blake Street. She stopped when she saw the street sign, and looked down the block towards the coffeehouse and the boutique. Perhaps, she thought, she needed to see this. Maybe watching the man she loved committing his heart, mind, body and soul to another woman was what she needed to see to find closure.

She ambled on, footstep after solemn footstep, toward the Roasted Renegade Cafe and Coffeehouse across from The Blake Boutique.

Lindsey walked in. The breakfast crowd was still in full force. Zoey was no where to be seen that morning.

Lindsey had no appetite, so she waited in line to order a mocha latte, the first of many that morning. She would sit at the table where she was always seated at until lunch time, and then she would somberly watch her dreams burn away into dreadful ash that would sting her eyes and scorch her soul.

Since the night that she had spoken to Zoey, she had not given any thought to what Zoey had told her she believed the table could do. Lindsey was far too rational minded to give any credence to such fantastical ideas. She believed in pain and longing; she believed in love, and loss - she did not believe in magical maple coffee shop tables.

There were moments in the next few hours that seemed to move painfully slow, while in some other ways, the time flew by. People came and went in the tables nearest to her, as they did through the whole cafe, but it was the ones closer to her that distracted her at times during her wait.

She found some amusement in a small family that sat in the table closest to her, enjoying their breakfast. A man and a woman in their early twenties - a couple of years younger than she was - were eating with their daughter, who looked between two and three years old. The couple themselves had more tattoos than she had ever seen on anyone before. The baby daughter was wearing a black mini-dress that said across the front of it 'My Daddy Loves me more than ZOMBIES love Brains!'

Lindsey, even in her despair, could not help but to smile at the writing on the little dress. The little girl watched Lindsey as she watched her, and smiled widely at Lindsey. Lindsey smiled back. She found it comforting to see a family of people so different from the type of world she'd grown up in to be such a normal and loving family.

When the couple with the little girl packed up and left, the father picked up the dishes and brought them up to the counter where the food was prepared. A fork had fallen from the edge of the tray between the wall and the table that Lindsey was sitting at. The man had not noticed the piece of silverware fall, but Lindsey did, although she couldn't find the will to speak to other people if it wasn't a necessity. She watched it fall; it almost seemed in slow motion, striking the hardwood and bouncing before coming to a stop out of the way against the wall. The sound of the fork striking the floor was muffled by the busy noise of the morning rush.

The hour of noon came at hand. The deep chasm that Lindsey had fallen into was unvaried despite the several mocha lattes she consumed that enabled her to keep her table. The caffeine agitated her already frayed nerves, but it did not alter her demeanor.

Once Upon a Wicked Eve

Mark came around the corner of Blake Street and Parke Street, heading for The Blake Boutique. Lindsey sat up in her seat, her eyes fixed on Mark as he approached the boutique's front door. She wanted to jump up and out of her chair and run across to him, but instead she stayed solidly glued to the spot she was in.

Mark and Stephanie came outside and sat at their regular bistro seats. Lindsey's heart began to race. Mark had carried the normal lunch bags as he always did, but Lindsey could see from her vantage point that Mark had slipped the white ring box he had shown everyone at the office out of the bag he had his lunch in below the table and onto his lap, out of Stephanie's view.

Lindsey's desperation was overwhelming all of the rational thinking she had ever known. She looked down, and reached to grab the fork that had fallen against the wall near the table. She grasped it tightly in her right hand, never taking her eyes off of Mark and the ring box. Mark's smile was beaming at Stephanie throughout the lunch hour while his finger nervously tapped on the box below the tabletop.

Lindsey scratched and scraped fiercely into the wood surface of the table. She didn't even look down, afraid that if she took her eyes off of the ring box, that would be the moment Mark pulled it into Stephanie's view. Then, it would all be over.

Mark gripped the box firmly, ready to pull it from below the bistro top when he suddenly froze. His expression changed from excited and nervous to a glazed over sort of look. Lindsey quickly looked down at the surface of the table where she had been scratching feverishly with the fork tine.

Sloppily, and almost incomprehensively, the words 'Mark loves Lindsey' were deeply engraved into the table's surface, far deeper than anything else written or scratched into the table's finish.

Lindsey's eyes opened widely, looking down at what she'd done. She quickly drew her gaze back up to Mark and Stephanie. Stephanie was looking at Mark with concern. Mark closed his hand around the ring box and stood up from his seat. Stephanie did as well, but Mark raised his hand as to stop her from getting up, said something else to her and turned to walk in the opposite direction. The look on Stephanie's face was one of hurt and confusion; she looked on helplessly as Mark rounded the corner out of her sight.

Lindsey sat bewildered in her chair. She suddenly felt a presence behind her, followed by Zoey's familiar voice as she pointed down with her black painted fingernail at the newest names on the mysterious table.

"*That*," Zoey remarked, "is probably not a good thing."

The weekend went by quietly for Lindsey in the solitude of her townhouse apartment. She was still not sure what she had truly witnessed as she watched the odd exchange between Mark and Stephanie in front of the Blake Boutique. There were a couple of things that she was sure of though. At least, there was what she believed.

One thing was that something came to Mark that had made him change his mind about proposing to Stephanie. Lindsey could not go back to the office on Friday because she herself had went home sick, so there was no way to know if anyone at the office had heard what had happened, or why.

The other thing that Lindsey knew, of course, was that it had nothing to do with carving her and Mark's names into the table at the Roasted Renegade. Zoey's crazy story about the table made no rational sense, no matter how much Zoey believed it had everything to do with what happened between Mark and Stephanie.

Lindsey came into work earlier than usual Monday morning. She was greeted politely by Liz as she came in, who asked her if she was feeling better this morning.

"Yes, I am, thank you," Lindsey replied, smiling and nodding her head.

The office space that Benson and Crane worked out of was mostly one large open loft divided into cubicles in front of large windows that overlooked a Lake Michigan bay from the third story of a three story building. There were a few private offices, but most of the real team work was done in an open environment full of computer screens and white boards and overhead projectors.

Lindsey moved on to her desk position in her little cubicle near the farthest end of the room from the office entryway. There were only two other people in the office besides Lindsey and Liz. She saw Mr. Benson, one of the two owning partners of the firm, walk out from his office to the coffeepot, fill his cup, and nod to her from across the room as he returned to his office.

The other person she could hear shuffling around at a desk, but she could not see that it was Mark until he popped his head up over the cubical wall. Lindsey looked away abruptly, ducking back down behind her cubical wall. She could hear footsteps walking in her direction from where she had seen Mark standing.

"Lindsey?" came Mark's voice, standing just behind her.

Lindsey swung around slowly in her chair and looked up at Mark. He was smiling, which Lindsey found strange given the last look on his face she had seen three days before on the street - a look of sadness and confusion, at least as she had remembered it being.

"Hiii," she said clumsily. "How are you, Mark?"

Mark's smile widened. "I'm alright," he said, his eyes echoing the clear morning sky like calm reflecting pools. "How was your weekend?"

"Um. Quiet. I stayed home all weekend. I had to leave work on Friday...I haven't been feeling well."

"Oh. I'm sorry. Yeah, I remember Liz saying that you'd left when I told her I was looking for you."

"You were looking for me? Why?" asked Lindsey.

"I...I wanted to talk to someone about...about Stephanie and I. I just thought you would be a good person to talk to," Mark stated, fumbling to get the sentence out right.

Lindsey cautiously sat up straighter in her chair. "What about you two? How did things go on Friday with the..." Lindsey paused, having trouble getting out the word, "Proposal?"

Mark's shoulders slumped. "Not well."

"I'm so sorry," lied Lindsey. "Did she say no?"

"No," said Mark. "I just couldn't go through with it." Lindsey's eyes widened and she could feel her cheeks go flush. She did manage to at least hold back a smile.

More people started coming into the office, doling out their morning greetings before breaking off into their various cubicles.

"Hey," Mark leaned in close to Lindsey. "Maybe here isn't the best place to talk. Do you think I could take you out to dinner later? Not a date, of course. I just broke up with Stephanie. But I'd really like to talk to someone, you know, not connected to Steph and I. Would that be okay?"

Lindsey gulped to herself. "Yeah. Yes. That's fine." She smiled. Mark returned the smile.

"Good. I'll get your address later and I'll pick you up around six-thirty," Mark said delightfully, and returned to his cubicle. He looked back twice at her as he made his way across the room.

Lindsey circled back around to her computer screen and slumped forward like the exchanged had knocked the wind out of her. *What is going on?* she thought. *He said they broke up - that it was he that broke up with her. Is this real?*

The rest of her thoughts of disbelief in the situation were overtaken by her thoughts of excitement and joy over finally getting to spend time alone with Mark. She would finally have her chance to let him see who she really was.

Mark picked Lindsey up exactly at six-thirty at her apartment like he said he would.

With the gesture of a true gentleman, he opened the passenger side door of his black 2015 VW Beetle for Lindsey and took her to the more uppity southwest side of town to the Bayfront Corridor Shops and Restaurants. Mugs Marina Tavern was the eatery of choice - a nautical themed, elegantly refined restaurant and bar that sat elevated overlooking the marina harbor where many of the most extravagant seafaring vessels in town were docked throughout the summer months.

The dinner conversation was light and friendly; Lindsey had always known that Mark had a quick wit and a good sense of humor, but had not expected how much he'd have her laughing through the evening and on into the night. After the meal, they walked out onto the docks where the big boats made their summer moorings. The night couldn't be more beautiful. The stars were starting to break through the waning afternoon light, and the air smelled fresh and sweet; the warm evening breeze had caught the scent of wildflowers from the distant hillside and carried their fragrance down across the bay.

It was then that Lindsey had realized that Stephanie's name had not come up once that evening. That was, after all, why he was taking her out tonight - to talk about what had happened between he and Stephanie. Although everything inside of her wanted to forget the subject, there was still a part of her that couldn't let it go.

"So," started Lindsey, turning away from the ever growing spectacle of stars in the evening sky, "what happened with Stephanie?"

"Ah," sighed Mark, looking off across the bay at the harbor lights twinkling from the western peninsula. "I can't explain it. I was ready. I know I was ready to pop the question, and suddenly...it just felt wrong. I couldn't do it. I called her later in the day and told her we needed space. But I knew...I knew it was over."

"Just...like that?" asked Lindsey, apprehensive and puzzled.

"Yes. Just like that. And...there was something else. You are going to think that this is strange," Mark said.

Lindsey immediately thought to herself that all of this was beginning to seem a little strange, despite the fact that she was enjoying herself a great deal in Mark's company.

"It's alright. I'd very much like to hear," she said, unsure if that statement was entirely true.

"Well," Mark started, uncomfortably, "the moment I knew that I couldn't go forward with Stephanie, thoughts of you came into my head and I just couldn't stop thinking about you. I came back to the office and you weren't there. I knew the office wouldn't give out your home address or phone number. I actually drove around town hoping that I'd see you walking on the street somewhere, just so I could talk to you."

In her heart, Lindsey was hearing all of the things that she'd ever wanted to hear from Mark; but in her mind - the same mind that discounted the idea of there being a magical maplewood table - that mind was telling her that everything about this that she wanted to feel so right felt so incredibly *wrong*.

Lindsey forced a smile to her lips, and Mark smiled in return. She had suddenly become aware that she had to get away from Mark for the night. It was then that something came to mind from the conversation that she had with Zoey the night she came to apologize to her. It was an escape plan.

"Well...I have laundry that I have to get done tonight. Early day tomorrow. I should probably get home," she fibbed to Mark.

"Oh. Well, do you need some help. I'm pretty good with an ironing board," he boasted.

She hadn't anticipated an eagerness to help with laundry...especially from a man.

"Um...no, thanks though," she replied. "There are a lot of...delicates."

Mark looked confused.

Lindsey took a more direct approach. "Panties. Bras. That stuff."

"Ah," said Mark, embarrassed. "Well, okay then."

He was obviously disappointed, but kept jabbering about whatever he could think of to talk about during the short ride back to Lindsey's apartment. He did not want the evening to end. He walked her to the door of the townhouse, keeping close to her as they approached the porch.

"I hope you had a nice night," he said, standing face to face with her under the bright moon that was now up high in the summer night sky.

Lindsey smiled a friendly smile before she noticed that he was moving his face in closer to hers. She froze, knowing everything about this was wrong, but she also had another thought. *What if this is the only time this might ever happen?*

She knew what was right, but in that moment she was going to do the wrong thing, and she was strangely okay with that.

Lindsey leaned in and kissed Mark back, deeply, passionately; it was the most intense feeling that Lindsey had ever felt. Time felt as if it had stopped, but only briefly. Lindsey pulled away, avoiding those eyes that still shimmered blue in the moonlight, rushed through her apartment door and locked it behind her.

Once she was inside, she took a few deep breaths before running upstairs and splashing cold water on her face. She peeked out the window of her bedroom and saw Mark standing beside his car. He paced back and forth before starting towards her door once more.

Shoot, she thought. Now what?

He stopped before he reached the door, and with much hesitation, turned back toward his car, got inside, and drove away.

Lindsey felt relieved that he had gone. She had no idea though what she would do next. Was Zoey right? Did the table have something to do with this? As much as it didn't seem possible, it was the *only* thing that made any sense.

The coffeehouse was closed, and she had no idea how to contact Zoey otherwise. She decided she would wait until lunchtime tomorrow and go to the Renegade to find her. Zoey was the only person she could think of that might have a clue how to undo what she had done.

Lindsey awoke the next morning to a knocking downstairs at her front door.

It was early, earlier than she normally would get up to get ready for work. She pulled herself up and looked out the bedroom window to the street in front of her apartment. When she saw the VW Beetle parked across the street in nearly the same spot it had been the night before, she quickly ducked back down, hoping that she had not been seen by Mark.

Lindsey scrambled to find her glasses. It was a strange feeling trying so hard to avoid him when up until the day before he was almost all she thought about. She tip-toed across the floor and waited until she heard the knocking continue. There were other people who lived in the building, and she wasn't sure if Mark was going to give up, so she reluctantly decided to answer the door.

Mark stood on the doorstep with a brown paper bag in his hand. He smiled a cheerful smile but his eyes look tired. He was exhausted.

"I brought you some bagels. They're from Krendler's Bakery on Kent Street. They make them daily. I don't even know if you like bagels, or what kind. I got a plain one, an everything one, and a chocolate one," he said excitedly.

"Mark," Lindsey said wearily, "it's six-fifteen in the morning. We don't have to be to work until eight-thirty." Lindsey looked up and down at the frumpled clothing he was wearing.

"Are those the same clothes you were wearing last night?" she asked.

Mark looked mildly embarrassed. "Yeah. I slept in the car last night."

"Why did you sleep in your car?" Lindsey asked, flabbergasted.

"After I left, I just drove around. I didn't want to go home. I don't know what it was. I just felt like I needed to be close to you. So, I slept here," he said, pointing to his car across the street. "I left just a short time ago to get breakfast. I thought maybe we could ride to work together?"

Lindsey exhaled slowly while she closed her eyes to gather her thoughts. She smiled at Mark, and said, "Thank you for the bagels, Mark. That was so sweet. I'll take them, but before you go into work you need to go home and take a shower. Maybe shave as well. Okay?"

"But...couldn't I just take a shower here?" He asked the question as if it were no big deal, like it was something that he did often.

"No! No...Mark, I don't think that would be a good idea right now," she said, and thinking quickly, leaned closer to Mark and whispered, "My mom came in late last night to surprise me. I don't think it would be all that appropriate for you to shower over today. Alright?"

"Oh, yeah, sure. I understand," he said, nodding, but Lindsey still wasn't sure he was completely onboard with her reasoning.

"Okay, then, I'll see you at work," she said, and quickly shut the door even as he was leaning in to give her another kiss.

She waited by the door until she was sure he had gotten into his car and driven away.

Once he was gone, she ran upstairs, cleaned herself up, brushed her teeth, threw on a t-shirt and jeans, wrapped a silk scarf over her head and put on a pair of oversized sunglasses like she had seen movie stars wear when they are trying to hide in plain sight out in public. She slipped over her clothes a three-quarter length burnt orange raincoat and grabbed the bag of bagels on her way out the door, setting out on foot to the Roasted Renegade, which was only six blocks from her apartment.

At six-thirty in the morning, there still weren't too many customers sitting down in the coffeehouse. Most of the patrons that had come in that morning were just in long enough to get their coffee to go, and out the door they went. Still, there were about a dozen people sitting down for a full meal, and that number would go up as the minutes ticked by.

Lindsey walked in the front door and glanced off to her left at the round table in the window alcove as she passed by. She shuddered slightly as a chill ran up her neck.

The girl at the counter was unfamiliar to Lindsey, a young girl of Asian decent whose nametag read 'Beth' across it in all capital letters.

"Good morning, how can I help you?" chirped Beth, all smiles.

Lindsey leaned towards Beth. "I need to get a hold of Zoey," she said, almost in a whisper.

Beth's smile disappeared from her face. "That girl kinda scares me. I have only worked here three weeks, and she worked a morning shift last week. I always work the morning shift. People say I have a bright and shiny disposition in the morning, so I always get to work it, but that girl is *not* a morning person."

Lindsey felt dumbfounded. "Yes, I understand what you are saying. But I need to talk to her. Do you know how to reach her?"

"We're not supposed to give out employee phone numbers to anyone. Ever. Company policy," Beth told her.

Lindsey frowned. Then, she remembered the fact that she was wearing huge, gaudy sunglasses, and started to fake-sob right there at the counter. Beth panicked, and not knowing what to do, grabbed some napkins from the counter and gave them to Lindsey, who took them to pretend dab the fake tears behind her glasses.

Beth whispered to her. "I suppose I can give her a call and tell her that you are here looking for her. Would that work?"

"Yes, yes, thank you so much," Lindsey said, giving the appearance of regaining her composure. "Tell her Lindsey needs to see her ASAP."

Beth nodded and flashed a quick, awkward grin as she moved toward the counter to get the phone. She examined a list of names and numbers from a tablet behind the counter, and dialed a number from the list. From the distance that Lindsey stood away from her, she could not hear what Beth was saying to Zoey, although Beth seemed extremely agitated and almost upset. She hung up the phone, and stepped over to where Lindsey was waiting.

Beth looked a little shaken when she first approached, but forced a smile and said, "Zoey said she will be down in about fifteen minutes, and for you to wait at your table."

Beth turned right around and went back to the counter without saying another word.

My table. She was afraid of that. She moved over to the table and sat where she had so often sat, and found it hard not to look at the names that she had engraved so deeply into its surface.

Lindsey moved her eyes up to the window and watched as the minutes went by. People walking to and from work and home, visitors coming in and out of the coffeehouse. Then she saw Stephanie slowly walking up to the locked front door of the Blake Boutique. Lindsey was suddenly overcome with a feeling of guilt over the lives and relationships that she had apparently now ruined.

She looked back down at the table top, but tried to avoid looking at the names she had added to its surface. It was then that she noticed something that she hadn't before in all the times she'd sat at that table.

It was faint, far lighter than any of the other etchings into the table. It appeared that at least once the table had been sanded down and resurfaced. Many names must have been expunged in the process, but this one name had been carved so deeply that it had not entirely been wiped from the face of the maplewood table.

Lindsey read the name 'Adrienne' out loud as she saw its outline thinly below the semi-gloss surface. She looked up from the name just at that moment to see Zoey standing outside the window looking in at her; Zoey's face was full of sadness and regret. She knew what it was that Lindsey had just come to realize.

Lindsey stood up from her seat and hurried out the front door of the Roasted Renegade. Zoey stood still, her head hung low, as Lindsey approached her. Lindsey stepped close, now face to face with the goth girl.

"Who is Adrienne?" Lindsey asked urgently.

"I told you," said Zoey, eyes still tipped to the sidewalk below. "She was a mistake."

"You carved her name into that table. That's how you knew what the table could do! It wasn't just from watching people in the coffee shop. You actually knew it because you did it yourself!" said Lindsey, her voice steadily rising in anger.

"No, I didn't..." started Zoey.

"Don't lie to me!" interrupted Lindsey. "Why did you even tell me about the table. Do you get off on seeing people get hurt? How could you be so cruel?"

Lindsey thought she could almost see flames flash in Zoey's eyes. Her face changed from a look of hurt to a hard, stony gaze.

"First of all," fumed Zoey, drawing the attention of a couple walking by up the block, who looked up and hastily changed their course, "I'm not sure what you did, but I can assume that things didn't go quite how you hoped they would. Am I right?"

Lindsey coyly nodded her head.

"Second, I was trying to help you. I told you that you shouldn't use the table. That you didn't need it. I even warned you what might happen if you did."

"And third - I have never carved a name into that table. It was Adrienne who carved our names into the table," Zoey revealed.

Lindsey slowly sunk down to the sidewalk and leaned herself against the brick window ledge of the coffeehouse. Zoey sat down beside her, her legs criss-crossed beneath her, facing Lindsey.

"I'm sorry I yelled at you," said Lindsey, her eyes now glassy.

Zoey looked on at her sympathetically. She lowered her head before saying, "I'm sorry too."

"I freaked out," said Lindsey, regretfully. "Mark was going to ask Stephanie to marry him yesterday at lunch. I couldn't help myself. I dug so deeply, so desperately into that table. I don't even think I believed anything would happen. That I would just look across the street and watch my dreams vanish into thin air. And now...now I wish they would have."

Zoey, cautiously and awkwardly, put her arm around Lindsey's shoulders. Lindsey's head fell down onto Zoey's shoulder as she started to cry harder now, and Zoey let her for as long as she needed.

After a few minutes, Lindsey's crying ceased. She lifted her head and looked at Zoey.

"I need you to tell me. What ended up happening with Adrienne? Is there a way to stop this? Mark is obsessed with me now. At first, I thought it might be ok. But I know that it's not. I have to make this right somehow," said Lindsey.

Zoey's face seemed to go a little whiter than her usual pallor. She turned her head away at first, then turned it back to Lindsey.

"Walk with me," said Zoey. "I'll tell you everything that I know."

Zoey had moved to town just a couple of years before. Born and raised a city girl, the small town life seemed a far cry from where she'd ever thought she'd find herself at this juncture in her life. A couple of years before she moved here, her parents had been the victim of a drunk driver who had ran through a red light at a busy intersection. Zoey, an only child, was left alone with few relatives around to help out after the funeral. She did however have a grandmother, her Grandma Clara, who lived in the small northern town (which was actually more like a small city on the shores of Lake Michigan), and her grandmother was having trouble living alone and taking care of the home that she lived in. Zoey made the decision to try and help her in whatever ways she could.

New places didn't come easy for Zoey. She loved the idea of traveling. She wanted to see the world some day, and as long as she was just passing through from place to place, she didn't have to put down roots; that meant she wouldn't have to go through the awkward social rituals associated with getting to know people.

This was not such an occasion. She would have to get a job. She would have to shop. She would be places where people may see her, again and again, and she would have to accept that. She had some life insurance money left from a policy that even her parents had forgotten about, so that gave her a transitional cushion to get acclimated with this new place that she would for now call home.

The Roasted Renegade was one of the first places she'd taken a liking to. It was the closest thing that reminded her of the city life, and the people who worked there, the baristas and the cook staff especially, seemed cool in all their own ways. Heavy on the tattoos, living to their own rhythm, and not afraid to express their own sense of individuality appealed much to Zoey. But there had been one girl working at the Renegade that found that same appeal and more in Zoey - the barista girl named Adrienne.

Adrienne was an attractive girl with a bright smile and even brighter green and platinum blonde hair. She had it cut very short along the left side of her head, about a quarter of an inch, and much longer on the right side, brightly dyed. She wore glasses that seemed almost too big for her face, and her ears were filled with silver rings and trinkets.

Everyday when Zoey came into the Renegade for coffee or food, Adrienne would make a point to be the one to wait on her. Adrienne was not shy, but she wasn't sure how to approach Zoey. She would make little compliments about how she looked on certain days, and tried small talk in an attempt to break through Zoey's passive demeanor, but Zoey showed little more than cordial attentiveness in response to Adrienne's efforts. Adrienne had heard rumors about the strange maplewood table, but she didn't really believe in it.

Still, one night when she closed down the coffeehouse, late in the evening, before the last light was turned out in the dining area, Adrienne looked on at the table and all its etchings in the dim light of the street through the alcove window.

She looked around through the window. There was no one to be seen walking the street at that hour on a week day evening. Adrienne took a flat headed screwdriver from a toolbox in the storage room and sat down at the table. She carved, lightly at first, the name Zoey and the name Adrienne, into the surface. Then, she thought that the names would show up better if she pressed harder a second time, and so she carved into the letters of each name again. This time, though, Zoey was heavy on her mind. She could see her in her thoughts, and the more she thought about her, the harder she pressed into the table.

Before long, she realized that Zoey's name and her name were the names carved the deepest into the table. She stopped, and then realized she hadn't put anything connecting the names into the table, so she then engraved a small heart in between the two names before turning out the last light that night and locking the coffeehouse doors.

The next day, Zoey was one of the first customers in the Renegade that morning.

Adrienne waited on her as usual, and Zoey was quiet as usual, but Adrienne noticed that there was something different about Zoey that morning.

As Zoey sat in a corner, far off in the back, she couldn't take her eyes off of Adrienne...

"...and I just couldn't take my eyes off of her," Zoey told Lindsey as they walked side by side across the waterfront park by the bay. "It was like nothing I'd ever felt before. It was so sudden. So intense. I didn't even question why I felt the way I did. I just had to see her."

"So what happened then?" asked Lindsey, fixated on Zoey's story.

"I went up to talk to her. I asked her if maybe we could get together when she was done working. Her face lit up and I just remember feeling nothing but joy in that moment. At least that's how I think I remember it. You can't ever clearly convey a feeling in simple terms. You just feel it, and you know it. She smiled and gave me her number, and I remember just walking the streets circling the coffeehouse from a distance until four o'clock when she got off her shift."

Zoey and Lindsey came to the walkway that extended out onto a long pier, housing several large boats, not as grandiose as the ones that surrounded Lindsey and Mark the night before, but still an impressive display. The morning air was fresh and cool, the harbor waters still placid. There was a hint of humidity growing in the air; the day would warm fast, and the midday air would be thick and uncomfortable.

Zoey continued. "We walked all over town, up and down the streets for hours, and we talked about everything we could think of. Growing up, feeling socially gawky and out of place. When evening came, it was beautiful. Calm and clear. A lot like this today, but very warm under the light of a heavy crescent moon hanging over the bay. I remember telling her how I felt like the moon was like a two pointed hook that hooked our hearts together. It was the corniest thing I can imagine, and I'm not even sure it made any sense, but she laughed anyway.

"It was right here, on the pier, the first time that I kissed her. She said that it was the first time that she ever kissed another girl." Zoey paused for a moment, looking out across the water of the bay. "I know I wanted more that night, but she slowed things down. That wasn't like me. It was like...a hunger. We stayed together late that night. She said she had to work early, so I walked her home, to a house up the hill on Green Street. I didn't want to leave her. After I walked away from the house, I stood down the block and watched a light come on upstairs in her house. I could see her silhouette, and then the light went out.

"I tried to go home and sleep, but I could not stop thinking about her. I finally did get some sleep, only for a few hours, and the first thing I did when I woke up was head to the coffee shop. Adrienne was there, and at first she seemed happy to see me, but at the same time, she looked at me oddly. I got my coffee and went off into the corner, and I stayed there for most of the day.

"When she finally got off of her shift, I told her I wanted to hang out with her, but she said she had plans to go shopping with her mother that afternoon. I felt totally empty when she said it, and asked her...no, I pleaded with her to change her plans. She had the same worrisome look on her face as she did when I showed up at the Renegade that morning."

"Did she change her plans?" asked Lindsey.

"No," Zoey flatly replied. "She told me she couldn't go with her mom another night that week, and that she would call me tomorrow. I left the coffeehouse and I came down here to the pier and I cried most of the night. Me. Crying. All night. It was crazy, but it was happening even so. She didn't call the next day. I went to the Renegade, but she wasn't there. Well, I found out later that she was, she'd just been avoiding me. She wasn't taking my calls, no matter how many messages I'd leave her..."

"Where is Adrienne?" Lindsey interrupted. "What happened?"

Zoey took a deep breath, and let it out with her eyes shut tight.

"She's dead."

Lindsey was dumbstruck by the words as Zoey uttered them.

"How?" Lindsey murmured. "How did she die?"

Zoey was obviously rattled revisiting memories that she wished to leave alone. It was something that she knew she had to bear. She felt a depth of responsibility for the situation Lindsey had now found herself in.

"Three days had gone by since I became so taken in by these feelings for Adrienne. She had avoided me most of that time, but I met up with her walking home that last night. I begged her to just talk to me. She finally said she would, and we walked down to the breakwall across the harbor. Clouds had been gathering through the afternoon and into the evening that night, and it had started to drizzle, but it was a warm rain. I thought, in my own way, that it was kind of a romantic rain. Romantic was not a word I was accustomed to thinking about, but it was heavy on my mind that night. I needed to show her that I truly cared for her, and that I was sorry for whatever it was that I did to drive her away. I remember all of these thoughts...all of these feelings. They seem so alien to me now."

"What do you mean, alien?" asked Lindsey. "How did they disappear?"

Zoey once more looked out from the pier, over the water to the breakwall.

"It's so calm this morning," she said. "Not like that night. We walked out to the end of the wall. Neither of us said much at first. The rain had begun to pick up, and she said that she wanted to go. I blocked her path, and begged her to talk to me. She told me that it was a mistake. She should have never used the table. I had no idea what she was talking about. I told her that I loved her. She said that I didn't even know her. That didn't seem to matter to me."

Zoey looked up into the sky. There were no clouds this morning. Only pale blue, vast and bright and beautiful.

"The clouds turned dark and vile. The rain crashed down on us and around us. The water turned as black as the sky. I was crying, pleading. She said there would never be anything between us. She said that she was sorry for everything. I think that she was crying too, but the rain was completely soaking us, so I couldn't tell for sure. The winds were heavy and strong, pushing the waves up over the stone breakwall. I dropped down to the concrete surface, a sobbing, rainsoaked mess. Adrienne walked quickly past me. I was watching her walk away when I heard a loud crash. I thought it was thunder at first, until I saw a huge swell of lake water tower over the side of the breakwall. In the darkness, it almost looked like a giant hand had reached up from the black waters and slapped Adrienne into the rocks lined up along the bank of the wall."

"Oh my God," Lindsey gasped, inadvertently drawing her hands up to cover her mouth. She felt horrified at the sad fate of the girl with whom she shared this one terrible thing in common.

"I tried desperately to get to her. She'd struck her head on the rocks, and when the lightning flashed, I could see her floating in the water. I could see where she was, but I couldn't reach her. I called 9-1-1 on my cell phone. The fire department was there within three minutes. The police were there just behind them. They recovered her body quickly, but it was too late to revive her. But...I already knew that..."

"What do you mean? How could you?" asked Lindsey.

"I knew she was dead the moment her head hit the rock. All I can tell you is...is that when I was trying to get to her, I was not trying to rescue the love of my life. All of the feelings that had consumed me for the past three days had vanished as soon as she went off the breakwall. I was trying to save a girl...a stranger that I happened to know a lot about. But that was all. The feelings were gone."

Lindsey stood by bewildered by the strange tale Zoey had shared with her. She stood alongside Zoey, peering across the way at the quiet breakwall, thinking about poor Adrienne.

Zoey turned to face Lindsey and this time did not lower her face. She looked eye to eye with Lindsey.

"This is all my fault. I'm sorry. I thought I could do something good for you. You seemed...you seem...I don't know. You're a good person. I came and asked for a job at the Renegade a few weeks after Adrienne died. I think some of the staff felt sorry for me. I came there just trying to understand who this person was, and why I had found myself so suddenly taken by her. I needed answers. Weeks went by, and I'd heard stories about Adrienne, but I still couldn't understand what happened. It wasn't until the fourth week that I'd been working there that I learned about the table. It was being taken to be resurfaced, and the manager on duty asked me to help carry it to the back door. I'd never even looked at it before...and then, I saw my name carved into the table, as well as Adrienne's. The manager I was helping saw it too, and then looked at me with what I can only describe as a long, awkward stare. He didn't say anything until we were outside, and then he told me the things he'd heard about the matchmaker table."

"The matchmaker..." Lindsey paused, considering the term's irony given what's ensued. "Did you believe him?"

"Not at first. But I watched, after the table came back to the coffeehouse, tucked away into its little alcove. I watched the people. I watched the exchanges, the suddenly love struck couples. I knew it was real then. I also saw that it wasn't all bad if it were used with a certain...moderation."

"Yeah," Lindsey frowned. "I get it. So, what happens now. I have to die to break Mark free from his obsession with me?"

Zoey shrugged. "I guess...or..."

"Or?" Lindsey narrowed her eyes at the goth girl.

"Or..." Zoey stated with a wicked grin. "We could try destroying that damn table. Sounds like more fun than dying, don't you think?"

Lindsey's phone buzzed every thirty to forty minutes throughout the day. It was always Mark's cell number, and she knew it was best not to answer the calls. She'd phoned Liz at work to let her know that she was taking a personal day. Being that the current project had been completed the prior day, there was no flack for taking the day off. The office had just signed a contract to work on promotional ideas for a local casino nightclub that was being developed, but it had been agreed that the new project wouldn't go forward until the current one had been completed. Mark was supposed to take lead on that one as well, but Lindsey knew that he was in no condition in his current state to take charge of anything.

Zoey brought Lindsey back to the home that she shared with her grandmother, half a mile from the downtown restaurant and business district of town. Zoey's grandmother would not be home for the next couple of nights; she and two friends had garnered enough playing points from the local casino that they had earned two overnight stays, dinner buffet passes, and free play at a sister casino seventy-five miles away. They had left just before Zoey got the call that Lindsey was looking for her at the Renegade.

Lindsey did not want to go back to her apartment that day. She was afraid if she went back, Mark would be waiting for her, although she knew at some point she would have to return to get her car later in the evening. Zoey didn't have a car of her own, and didn't need one normally. She would either walk to work each day, or if need be, take her grandmother's Ford Escape. Grandma was elected driver for this casino trip, so the Escape wasn't available, and if she and Lindsey were going to move that table, they were definitely going to need a vehicle.

Zoey had to close the Renegade that night, and went into work at 3 p.m. The coffeehouse was open until nine o'clock that Tuesday night, and it would be only Zoey and one kitchen staff person there cleaning up and shutting things down after the doors were locked. Zoey had been trusted as a closing manager for almost a year now, so there was a little bit of guilt for what she and Lindsey were going to do later that night. But Zoey felt an even greater guilt for what she had helped get Lindsey into with the cursed table. She was ready to accept whatever punishment she may have coming to her in the course of helping her friend.

The time ticked by slowly though the day for Lindsey, sitting in a strange house surrounded by unfamiliar things.

Most of the house had a northern country decor feel to it, white paneled walls trimmed out with denim blue moldings. It was clear that this was the part of the house inhabited by Zoey's grandmother. In almost every direction you looked, be it the living room or the kitchen, there were pictures, wall hangings, and even small decorative knick-knacks modeled after bird cages. Lindsey noticed the scent of eucalyptus in the air.

There was a bedroom and a bathroom in the lower level of the house, both used by Zoey's grandmother. Grandma Clara could not get up and down the stairs without great effort any longer, Zoey told Lindsey, so Zoey made the upstairs her living quarters. If Lindsey needed to use the restroom, she could go up the stairs and down the hall to the end and use Zoey's. Zoey didn't feel right about anyone going into her grandmother's private rooms.

When Lindsey did finally need a bathroom visit, she walked up the stairs and past the two upper level bedrooms. The first room she walked by was evidentially Zoey's bedroom. Her door was only half closed, and Lindsey couldn't help but to peek inside.

The trim in Zoey's room was the same as the rest of the house, which was in contrast to the rest of the decor in the room. Things were surprisingly neat and orderly, without clutter or messiness. Lindsey smiled to herself seeing this. She didn't really know what she expected as far as Zoey's sense of order, but the other things that she had noticed - the black lace curtains, the candles and jewelry on the dresser, the post-punk band posters on the walls - these things she imagined she might see.

She also saw several pictures of Zoey with whom she believed to be her parents. A few of the photos hung on the wall, with the exception of one especially sweet photo in a frame on Zoey's dresser alongside the only white candle in the entire room. The picture was of Zoey, Lindsey guessed between eight and ten years old, with her mother and father at an amusement park, all three of them with smiles from ear to ear, arms wrapped tightly around one another.

Lindsey smiled once again as she looked at the photograph, and then realized she had inadvertently wandered farther into the room than she intended. She backed out, and continued down the hall to the bathroom, getting distracted once again when she saw into the open doorway of the second bedroom upstairs.

This room had many cardboard boxes stacked along one wall, but what really caught Lindsey's attention the most was the multitude of painting supplies that filled the room, as well as the canvas oil paintings and watercolors that were scattered on the floor, leaning up against the walls. The floor was protected by a white sheet, tattered with paint. Beneath the cloth sheet was a large plastic drop cloth to further protect the carpet underneath, extending beyond the edges of the sheet.

Two of the pieces of art that Zoey had created drew Lindsey's attention the most. There was a full color oil painting that looked almost identical to the photo she had seen on Zoey's dresser in her bedroom. It was beautifully touching, and done with such depth and detail, reflecting how much of Zoey's heart she had put into it.

The other painting that Lindsey found, full of another kind of emotional profoundness, was the watercolor sitting upon the easel, painted in blacks, whites and shades of grey. It was from the perspective of a high boardwalk tower overlooking the waterfront area by the bay where she and Zoey had been that very morning. It was slightly abstract, but

Lindsey could clearly see the pier that they had walked out on as they talked, and in the distant background she could make out the breakwall, the same one that Zoey and Adrienne had been on the night that Adrienne died.

Lindsey suddenly felt guilty for snooping around, even though the door to the painting room had been wide open. She felt awestruck by the talent that Zoey had for painting; there was so much emotion and elegance in the work she had seen in the room. Lindsey stepped backwards out of the room and knocked over a large sketchpad that was leaning against the wall just inside of the doorway. The sketchpad tipped on its side and opened wide on the floor.

Lindsey's eyes widened when she saw the charcoal drawing on the open page of the sketchbook in front of her. She knelt down beside it to take a closer look at what she was seeing. There was so much detail; the lines in the individual hairs on the head, the shape of the eyes behind the dark framed glasses, the curves of the lips. Lindsey was almost in a state of disbelief as she looked upon a perfect drawing of herself on the page before her. She couldn't say how long she stared at the picture, and finally realized that she was blushing at the gesture of being the subject of the piece. She finally closed the sketchbook and returned it to its place against the wall before leaving the room.

Lindsey turned her phone off for several hours when the calls from Mark had not slowed down. She didn't turn it back on again until nearly eight o'clock, expecting a text from Zoey indicating when she should start walking to her apartment to get her car.

Lindsey hoped her disguise would hold up as she walked the streets home. She expected that Mark may be driving around looking for her, so she was trying to be as stealthy as possible.

The text came from Zoey at a quarter after eight. Lindsey would walk home and get her car, and then drive to the parking lot down the alley behind the Roasted Renegade. There she would wait until Zoey came down to get her after the kitchen helper left for the night, and they would go and get the table, put it in Lindsey's trunk, and take it to a place far out of the way outside of town.

Lindsey made it to her apartment without any problems, and with no sign of Mark. She drove a late model Buick sedan, and was concerned how the table was even going to fit in the trunk of the car. There was one other thing that Zoey told Lindsey to pick up. Lindsey drove to a gas station near on the edge of town and bought a two-and-a-half gallon gasoline can, filled it, and secured it in the trunk. She then continued on to the alley parking lot and waited.

There were very few cars in the parking lot at that hour. Lindsey sat nervously, anxious as to what the night would hold. But there was something else she was feeling, and it came as quite a surprise to her. She was feeling *alive*. She had a sense of excitement that she hadn't had for as long as she could remember, if ever had she felt it before. So many things, so many possibilities, seemed awakened within her. Breaking and entering, theft, supernaturally cursed tables...things that she could have never seen herself doing, and things that she could have never imagined existing, were now a very real part of the world in which she lived. Something was stirring deep within her, a hunger to taste and touch the promises and mysteries of a strange new world.

As her mind wandered, Lindsey was startled by the sudden knock on her passenger side window. She jumped, then looked to the window to see Zoey staring in at her, waving her hand from side to side as if to say 'Hello? Anybody home?'.

Lindsey got out of the car, and closed the door quietly.

The two girls walked briskly back to the rear door of the Renegade, up a short flight of metal steps beside a dumpster used by the café. Zoey had not yet locked the door, and the two stepped in from the alley and shut the door behind them.

From the back door of the coffeehouse, looking across the dining room at the obstacles that they had to maneuver the table around, it seemed an almost insurmountable task. The table was going to be too heavy for the two girls to lift over the other tables and carry across the room. They would have to find a way to roll it, a few steps at a time, around the other tables. Lindsey re-tied the scarf around her head, just in case someone walked by on the street and looked in the front window as they were moving the table. Zoey didn't bother, being that she worked at the coffeehouse, she could explain away her being there easy enough.

They started to move some of the tables that were closest to the front alcove out of the way. There was a sudden wrapping at the window of the coffeehouse. Zoey and Lindsey both jumped, startled by the sudden clamor

They froze, like an animal in the road caught in headlights, staring at the figure in the window looking in at them. There was a confused wave of the hand from the figure, and Lindsey realized that it was Mark looking in at the two of them.

Lindsey looked to Zoey, who had nothing more than a blank expression on her face, not knowing what they should do now. Lindsey looked back to Mark, and not wanting him to attract attention by staring in through the window from Blake Street, rushed over to the window where Mark was standing.

Mark raised both of his hands palms up, mouthing *'What are you doing?'* through the glass.

Lindsey pointed at him mouthing *'You'*, moved her finger pointed down in a circular motion *'Go around'*, then thrusting her thumb up and over her shoulder, pointing behind her *'To the back door'*.

Mark nodded that he understood, and rushed away from the window to circle around the building.

"What are we going to do?" whispered Zoey.

"We are going to use his help," replied Lindsey. "Right now, he would do whatever I ask him to do. If this actually works, then by the end of the night, it won't matter anymore." Zoey nodded in agreement.

The two girls hastened to the back door to get Mark inside, out of sight from anyone who might stroll by in the alleyway.

"Mark," Lindsey whispered, "What are you doing here? How did you know where I was?"

"I was driving around all day looking for you, and then I thought I saw your car at the gas station across town. It took some looking after that, but I happened to see you through the window as I drove up the street. What are you doing here, Lindsey? I've been trying to call you all day. I was so worried. Why didn't you pick up? Are you okay?" Mark went on, almost frantically. He still looked as if he hadn't gotten any rest whatsoever in the past twenty-four hours.

Lindsey seemed dumbfounded as to how she should respond to the barrage of questions. Her mouth fell open slightly, and she looked to her side at Zoey, who was already glaring at her, wondering how she would respond as well.

"Um," started Lindsey, "My phone is broken, and I took a day off to help my friend...move a table. But it's far too heavy for the both of us. Will you help?"

Mark lit up, feeling needed by Lindsey. "Sure. Yeah, of course I'll help." Lindsey smiled and looked at Zoey, who was not smiling until Lindsey made a motion with her eyes, nudging her head in Mark's direction. Zoey caught on and forced a fake smile, directing it at Mark.

Zoey and Lindsey tipped the table top towards them. The weight of the base of the table could easily be felt even with just tipping the table on its side, but Mark was determined to be the hero of the hour and lift the base off the floor, which he did, although the two girls could tell it was not without great effort. The three of them lifted the table above the other tables in the dining room and navigated their way to the back door and down the steps into the alley. Zoey stopped momentarily to lock the door behind her, and they continued to carry the table to Lindsey's car.

The trunk popped, and the three of them tried several different approaches to fit the table in the trunk, but nothing seemed to be working. Finally, Mark had a suggestion - one that they had wished he'd made far sooner.

"My truck is parked up around the block on Blake. We could just throw it in the bed to haul it wherever you need," he said, matter of factly.

Mark retrieved his truck, a 2009 Chevy extended cab pick-up, and drove it slowly down the narrow alleyway to the parking lot where Zoey and Lindsey waited with the table. The bed of the truck easily held the table; the three of them slid it in between the wheel wells upside-down. Lindsey grabbed the gas can from her trunk and placed it in the truck bed next to the overturned table, and then Mark, Lindsey and Zoey piled in the front seat of the truck and started up the alley toward Parke Street.

"I didn't know you had a truck, too," remarked Lindsey to Mark.

"I've had this for a couple of years now. I used to haul things for my uncle..." Mark had started before being cut off.

"Wait!" Zoey blurted out, suddenly. At that moment they were rolling slowly past the rear door of the Renegade.

Zoey jumped down from the truck, ran up the steps to the rear door of the coffeehouse and kicked the door hard, busting the door frame as the door flew open. She turned and came back down from the door and jumped into the truck.

"Okay," she said calmly, catching her breath. "We can go now."

Lindsey and Mark both sat looking at Zoey as she faced forward, staring through the front window of the truck. The look on Mark's face was one of utter confusion, while Lindsey just held a wide grin from ear to ear.

Zoey gave Mark directions out of town along a dirt road, then pointed to a left turn down a two track where they went on for another ten minutes before coming into a large sand pit.

The Pit, as it was called by the local teens who often partied there on the weekends, was well out of the way so it didn't attract a lot of attention when people gathered there. There were only two roads in and out of the sandpit, which itself was about one-hundred feet in diameter. It had been a while since Zoey had last been there, but it had not changed all that much.

She had gone to a couple of parties when she first moved in with her grandmother, but decided quickly that hanging out with a pack of wild drunken teenagers was not a fun, or wise, idea. She was obviously old enough to drink, although she rarely ever did, but if there was a police raid on the Pit, she was certain she would get nailed for providing alcohol to minors, even if she had not done so.

There was no one anywhere around the Pit on a Tuesday night, so it was a perfect spot for what they had come all the way out there to do.

Mark pulled the truck into the center of the sandpit and turned the engine off. Lindsey, Zoey and Mark got out of the truck, and Mark lowered the tailgate. They easily slid the tabletop off of the tailgate, with Lindsey and Zoey giving the table an extra nudge as it flipped off the back of the truck, causing the table to land squarely on its base with a little wobble.

Zoey and Lindsey stood silently, looking down at the table for several seconds before Mark finally asked, "Does anyone want to explain to me why we drove this table out into the middle of this sand pit?"

Zoey and Lindsey, turning their heads at once toward Mark, simultaneously responded "No."

Lindsey grabbed the gas can out of the back of the truck.

"You'd probably better move the truck away from the table," Lindsey told Mark.   Mark hopped back into the truck and moved it to the edge of the pit, pointing the nose of the truck down the path that they had arrived on.

Lindsey unscrewed the nozzle from the gas can and started pouring the contents of the can over the round maple surface of the table. When half of the gasoline was out of the can, Lindsey stopped.

"Your turn," she told Zoey, handing her the can. Zoey emptied the rest of the can's contents onto the table. The bright light of the full moon that night made the gasoline glisten across the tabletop. It seeped into the many scratches, nicks and deeper carvings as it flowed across the surface, dripping from the edges into tiny wet spots in the sand.

Zoey pulled a book of matches from her pocket. She looked up at Lindsey and Mark to see that the three of them were forming a triangle around the table.

Zoey turned to Lindsey. "You're absolutely sure this is what you want?"

Lindsey turned to look at Mark, who looked skeptically back at her. She turned her face back to Zoey, and without saying a word gave Zoey a quick double nod.

"Better stand back," warned Zoey. Mark and Lindsey stepped several more feet back, while Zoey stayed closer to toss the matches before she moved to a safe distance.

Zoey lit one match, then used the one to light the entire matchbook. The book flared brightly. Zoey drew her arm back and snapped the matchbook like a Frisbee toward the gasoline soaked table. As soon as the flames kissed the fumes, there was a bright, hot flash that engulfed the tabletop.

Zoey took several steps back from the burning table. All three of the onlookers stood by transfixed as the flames danced and twisted up from the maple table top.

Suddenly, the fire erupted ten feet high from the table surface with a sound that resembled a deep roar from some large, ferocious animal.

Zoey, Lindsey and Mark all jumped backwards; Mark almost lost his footing, stumbling further away from the fire. Zoey looked back and forth from Lindsey to Mark, not knowing what was happening. Gasoline was extremely flammable and explosive, but this was something different. This seemed *unnatural*.

Sparks started flying from the table in all directions. The wood began to pop and snap, and there were noises coming from it that sounded like screams as air escaped from places unseen. The flames were getting hotter and hotter, forcing the three of them to push further and further back away. The heat was actually causing the cast iron shaft to buckle beneath the burning tabletop, which was now starting to bubble and pop like thick liquid brought to a boil.

Pieces of the table, both burning solid and hot liquid, burst from the table and landed like hot embers several feet away before dissolving into nothing in the sand. Then there was a new, deeply disturbing thing that enamated from the blaze before them all.

The flames, the ones closest to what remained of the surface of the table, were changing and forming, first like the negative images of old cameras, them into clearly defined faces that lasted for only a few seconds before disappearing into the black smoke lost in the darkness.

Most of the faces none of the three of them recognized. There were a few that Zoey did recognize. People that she'd seen over time at the Renegade. She saw Derek's face, from 'Derek loves Tracy', form and fall into blackness. It was the next face that shook her the most. She could see Adrienne's face in the flames, the stranger, the obsessed infatuation, the love-struck girl, there in the fire and then gone forever in the darkness.

Lindsey stared on into the flames as well, looking through the march of face after face of all those that the table had stolen a little piece of their souls for the promise of love and devotion. And then, she saw Mark's face, and so did Zoey. Lindsey stared at Mark's face in the flames as Zoey turned to look at Mark's real face where he stood in the sand on the far side of the fire.

As Lindsey watched the face in the fire vanish, Zoey watched Mark's expression change into the glazed over, startled and confused look that she knew all too well. It was the same expression she had seen on her own face, reflected in the black waters when the lightning flashed on the night she reached desperately to try and save the girl who'd she herself had been completely enthralled with up until the moment that that girl's life had ended in the rocky waters beside the breakwall.

A final flash and roar, far greater than the first one, knocked Lindsey, Mark and Zoey all to the ground a few feet back from where they had been standing. The fiery cloud of black, yellow, orange and red rolled twenty-five feet into the air before collapsing back into itself and falling down to the ground, resting in what still glowed there in a pile of melted, red hot cast iron. The only sound left to hear was the hissing of the hot and soft metal surrounded by glassy sand two feet around where the iron base had stood.

Zoey sat up and breathed rapidly for a moment before getting her bearings. She looked over to the other two people with her there on that night.

Mark pushed himself up from lying on his back. The look on his face was one of complete bewilderment. Zoey could only imagine what was going through his mind at that moment. She heard to her right what she thought at first was a cough or a choke, and looked in the direction that Lindsey had been knocked down into the sand.

But it was not a cough, or a choke. Lindsey was sitting up, and she made the sound in a short burst again before erupting into hysterical laughter, rolling back over onto her side as she laughed. Zoey looked at Mark then, who was looking at

Lindsey as if she had lost her mind. Zoey then looked back at Lindsey and started laughing with her, almost uncontrollably. She rolled over in the sand as well and looked up into the full moon's light and smiled an exceptionally bright and satisfied grin.

She knew that Lindsey had not in fact lost her mind. No. Lindsey had finally found her *self*.

Six weeks had passed by since the night in the Pit.

In those weeks, Mark had worked very hard to repair the damage done to his relationship with Stephanie. It took a lot of begging, and promising, and enrollment in several months of couples therapy, but in the end they worked things out. She finally did get her ring, and she said yes, and blah-blah-blah, happily ever after. Mark never knew what that night in the Pit had truly been about, and most likely he would not have believed Lindsey and Zoey if they had told him, but he never asked. In fact, he did not utter a single word the rest of that night to the girls. He only drove them back to Lindsey's car, and then he sped away into the night.

When Zoey had went into work the day after the great table heist, she fully expected the police to be there waiting for her to haul her off to the county jail for questioning.

To her delighted shock and surprise, all she saw when she arrived was a carpenter fixing the broken door frame that she had kicked in the night before. The idea to kick in the door came as a last minute attempt to make it look like a breaking and entering, although in the back of her mind, she never really thought anyone would believe someone would break in just to steal a maplewood table.

She walked in through the back door and saw the head manager filling out paperwork at the coffee bar.

"What happened to the door?" she asked him as she slowly walked by.

He looked up from his paperwork, his eyes following her as she passed.

"Do you remember what time you got out of here last night?" he asked.

"I clocked out at ten," she told him. "So, ten I guess."

The manager grunted. "Some kid musta ran by and thought it would be cute to kick the door in. If the boss wants to file a police report, I can at least tell him it was after ten p.m."

Zoey looked over toward the window where the matchmaker table had always sat since the day she first set foot in the Roasted Renegade. There was another table sitting there now, one from the main dining floor, and the other tables around the floor were spread out just a little bit more than they usually had been.

No one throughout the entire day, or any day after, breathed a word about the table's disappearance.

Lindsey went into work the day after the strange night in the Pit, not knowing what to expect from Mark. When he finally came into the office, he went straight to his desk with little interaction from anyone else in the office.

The office manager, Jordan Craig, called a morning meeting, and all of the staff members gathered in a large open area away from the cubicles. There was no table to gather around here, just the chairs that were pulled from the cubicle desks.

"First and foremost, before we start on this casino thing, I want to congratulate Mark on the superb job he did leading the team on the hotel project," Jordan stated, leading the gathered group in a hearty applause for Mark.

Mark smiled and nodded as those closest to him shook his hand.

"Thank you, so much," Mark said, and then paused, looking to Lindsey, who at once felt the air leave her lungs. "Actually, I know everyone here worked really hard to do their parts to make this happen. What many of you may not know is that I consulted Lindsey on several thoughts I had, and it was her input that got the wheels rolling on many of the implemented project ideas."

Once again, applause filled the room, and this time, it was for Lindsey. She smiled, and silently mouthed the words *thank you* to Mark across the group. Mark smiled and nodded back to her. Soon after the recognitions were over, the group jumped right into a brainstorming session for the casino club project. It didn't take long for Lindsey to interject, "I have some ideas for that."

And that was how it started. Lindsey spouted off great idea after great idea, watching the nodding heads and pleasantly surprised reactions of her co-workers, many of whom were not even sure of what her name was before that day. It didn't take long before Lindsey was put on team lead of the project, the first of many projects that would eventually take her to the position of office manager and head project leader down the road.

Now here it was, six weeks gone by. Zoey had come in to open up the Renegade on that morning, and she was almost ready to be done with another long yet satisfying day at the best place that she had ever worked.

Zoey's temperament had changed over the last several weeks, and those who worked along side of her had noticed the dark veil had seemed to have lifted from the oft cynical goth girl. Most of them rather enjoyed working alongside of her during her shifts, whereas before, behind her back, straws were often drawn to trade shifts to not have to work with her. It wasn't that she created problems. She just scared the hell out of them. Zoey knew about the straw thing, she just didn't care. It amused her. But now, the tide had turned and it amazed almost everyone how much her glow seemed to fill the room.

She was still the 'goth girl'. She still enjoyed putting a little fear into new employees and into irritating customers. Only now, the *friends* she worked alongside were in on it with her.

Lindsey walked in through the front door of the Roasted Renegade around four-thirty, instinctively glancing to her left where the table once stood that cause so much grief. Its replacement sat there harmlessly with three teenage girls giggling around it while sipping iced mocha lattes.

Zoey looked to the door and saw Lindsey walking toward the counter, appearing as she had over the last several weeks.

Lindsey was wearing a red and black sleeveless summer dress that came down to just below her mid thigh. Her hair had escaped its customary ponytail, instead hanging with its slight natural curl to her shoulders and along the sides of her face. There was a streak of purple and red dyed hair that came down from the top of her head and ran along down the right side of her face. She was wearing make-up, and she walked with a new confidence that she had not had before the night the matchmaker table burned away into the shadows.

It was not only the table that had faded into the darkness that night. It was also the fears that held Lindsey back from allowing herself to let go and take control of her life.

Her fate.

Her destiny.

It was all her own now. All it took was a little larceny, and little dark magic, and the fearlessness and bravery of another who did not even realize how brave she was.

Lindsey walked to the counter, smiling at the goth girl.

"You almost ready?" Lindsey asked.

"I just have to clock out," Zoey replied, looking to the girl named Beth beside her at the counter. Lindsey remembered Beth from the day she came looking for Zoey when she had to hide from obsessive Mark.

"You alright for the rest of the afternoon, or did you need me to stay longer?" Zoey asked Beth.

"No, I'll be fine," she smiled. "You go on."

Zoey walked into the office to clock out, and walked around the counter to where Lindsey had stood waiting for her. Lindsey leaned in and gave Zoey a quick kiss on the lips, catching Zoey momentarily by surprise. Zoey enthusiastically returned the kiss.

The two grasped each other by the hand and walked through the rear door of the Roasted Renegade Cafe and Coffeehouse, together embracing the warm and wondrous essence of life, vast and infinite in its possibilities, beneath the calm and clear September sky.

Rick Jurewicz

The Crossroads Gambit

Everyone in the music world knows the legend. The one about the not-so-talented young man by the name of Robert Johnson, a man with big dreams who wanted to be the best bluesman the world had ever known.

There are many variations of the story, but the most popular one tells a tale of Johnson taking his guitar to a crossroads at midnight and meeting a large man who he believed to be the Devil himself. Johnson handed the Devil his guitar. The Devil tuned it and played a few songs before handing it back to Johnson. And with that subtle exchange, a deal had been struck. When the guitar was returned to his hands, Johnson had become the master of the instrument.

Over the next few years, Robert Johnson sowed the seeds of his own legend. In part, it was because of the incredible music that he had produced, recording only 29 songs in the year before his death at the young age of only 27, planting the earliest seeds of what would eventually become rock 'n' roll.

And then, of course, there was the story of his deal with the Devil…

Leland Graves knew the story all too well. He had big dreams too. He was already a moderately talented guitar player and singer, but things just weren't taking off as fast as he would have hoped. He was only nineteen. The year was 1979. He had seen many of his childhood rock idols rise and fall from fame. He had put together a theory at a very young age, catching on before many others would eventually as the years sailed past.

Hendrix. Jim Morrison. Janis Joplin. All dead at 27, like Johnson. Did they make the same deal? All of these shooting stars were some of the best of their kind, and they burned out all too soon.

Leland was going to be smarter than that. He wanted it all, but he would somehow find a way to best the Devil. This is what was on his mind when he found himself wandering down a lonely country road toward an isolated crossroads on a warm summer night in July.

It was nearly midnight when he arrived where Lilberry Lane and Rothbury Road converged on the outskirts of the small Midwestern town Leland had grown up in. Each corner at the crossing was the corner of a different farmer's land that went on for miles and miles out of sight. To the north and the south, the crop was corn. To the east, the farmer had a potato farm. The west field had all manner of different vegetable crops.

The moon was nearly full, so even in the darkness of the hour there was a bit of illumination that gave Leland an even greater sense of the stark stillness in the air that night. He was familiar with this crossroads, having spent some time a year or so before dating the potato farmer's teenage daughter. It did not end well when the farmer chased Leland out of the girl's bedroom window late one August night. He had not been back by this intersection since.

Leland found a thick section of a log lying beside the road that most likely had been a large chunk of unsplit firewood that had fallen off of a truck as it passed through the intersection. He righted the log; it was an even right-angle cut on both ends, and he sat himself down upon the log and stared off across the distance as he listened to the unnerving silence around him. There was no wind. There wasn't even the irritating sound of a cricket chirping or a whippoorwill from the trees on the edge of the distant woodlands. There was nothing at all.

Leland didn't know what he was supposed to do. He arrived at that spot with intent in his heart, but even he knew that the intent was tainted by his desire to somehow best the Devil at his own game. *Maybe that was what was keeping the beast away*, he thought. He sat upon his stump and pulled a pack of matches from his jacket pocket. The boredom was getting the best of him.

He struck a match, and he brought it up in front of his face, only inches beyond the tip of his nose, and he watched it slowly burn down to just above his fingertips before blowing it out. He tossed the spent match into the dirt on the road and pulled a second match from the pack, and he struck it. Once more, the flame burned down and as it did, Leland swore he could almost see it dance as it slowly sunk down into its own tiny death. This one almost singed the tip of his thumb and index finger milliseconds before he extinguished it with no more than a whisper of breath.

He pulled a third match and lit it aflame. As he brought it even with his eyes, a sudden wind, warmer than the still night air, pushed the flame sideways and snuffed it out of existence. The smoke was swaying upward in the moonlight, holding a soft glow as it rose above and beyond Leland. It was then that

Leland thought his eyes were deceiving him. A figure appeared to be standing in the semi-darkness through the smoke of the dead flame, straight ahead in his line of sight. He dropped the match and rubbed his eyes, but when he opened them again, the figure was most certainly standing there before him.

Leland leapt up from the log as the figure slowly began to move in his direction. His heart was beating so fast he thought it may actually come right out of his chest. He froze in his footsteps and felt the terror run through him as the shadowy figure began to come into focus in the pale light of the moon. Leland's jaw slowly dropped.

It was a woman, almost Leland's height with long, curly reddish-orange hair that hung well past her shoulders. Her hair looked wild in the moonlight, almost like flames licking up around slowly burning embers. Even in the dim light he could see that her eyes were dark, perhaps a dark brown hue, and the moonlight reflected in tiny red pinpricks in the pupils. She was wearing a long dress that was black with red flower blossoms scattered about it from head to toe. She walked barefoot on the hard gravel, but it didn't seem to bother her one way or the other. The dress had thin straps, and her arms were bare and sleek and long. She was, in his eyes, a truly beautiful creature in every sense of the word, and her presence alone on the dark road caught him off guard.

The woman stepped closer to Leland and she smiled a wide smile. He tried to think of something to say to her, but he found himself clumsy in all manner of speech in that moment.

"Hello, Leland. I expected a more enthusiastic greeting being that you made your way all the way out here on this gorgeous evening," she said to him, stretching her arms out wide and slowly twirling herself around as she looked up into the night sky from the center of the crossroads.

Leland's confusion was immediately obvious to both himself and the woman. She stopped her spinning motion and looked dead-on at Leland. "You wanted to see me, Leland," she said. Leland wasn't sure if it was meant to be a question or a statement, and the tone in which she said it didn't help matters.

"Are you…are you the Devil?" he asked, rather clumsily.

She gave him a serious stare for several seconds before finally bursting into laughter. "Oh, you silly people," she said. "No, I'm not *that guy*. HE isn't even what your kind think he is. 'Prince of Darkness' and all that. Things aren't quite like the stories you've been told. At least those *really old* stories. It's a different kind of arrangement. I'm more of an independent contractor."

"You're what…what does that mean?" asked Leland, dumbfounded.

"It means that we are both here because we both want something, and I think that we both have the power to give the other what they want," she said, moving in closer now to him. She brought her hand up to the lapel of his black jacket and ran her fingertips along its edge. She looked him up and down seductively, and brought her hand up to the side of his face, gently brushing his cheek with her soft fingers.

"My, my. You are certainly a handsome…devil, yourself," she said in a flirtatious tone of voice.

"Th…thank you," Leland muttered back. "What do you want?" he asked her.

"What. Do. I. Want," she said, stepping away from Leland and walking away a few feet before turning around to face him again. "Let's start with you, Leland Graves. You came here wanting. Tell me what you want."

Leland looked down at the ground for a long moment, and then gave the woman a deeply serious look directly into her dark eyes.

"I want it all. I want to be one of the biggest rock stars that the world has ever seen," he told her.

"Haven't you been practicing?" she asked him, with an obvious hint of sarcasm.

"That's not how the world works," he said bitterly. "It doesn't matter how hard you work, or even how good you are. It's about who you know. I can give them the best damn music that ever reached their ears, but that doesn't matter. They want more, and I don't have it. I need help."

"My help," she asked. This time, it sounded more like a question, although he still wasn't quite sure.

"What can you do?" asked Leland.

"Leland, I can give you everything you desire. You can be the star that you want to be. People will love both you and your music. Fame, fortune – they can be yours for the taking. All you have to do is say that you want me to help you," she said to him.

Leland swallowed hard. He still didn't know the cost of the deal, only that this strange woman in the night had just assured him that she could hand him his dreams. He knew, more than anything that he had ever known, that achieving this success was everything that he had ever dreamed.

"I," Leland started, with only a moment of hesitation, "I want you to help me."

A wide smile came to the woman's face. "Excellent!" she said, although there was an unsettling hiss that coincided with the exuberant joy that encircled the word like a heavy fog.

"What do I need to do now?" asked Leland. "Is that it? Just say I want your help?"

"Oh, there is always the fine print, as they say," she told him, suddenly revealing a rolled up piece of heavy paper not much larger than the palm of her hand. "For every bargain, there are terms. You will have your fame and fortune. You will have the love of the masses. All of that will be yours. However you spend the wealth you gain, all will be yours, and, if you play your cards right, you will have your place in history."

"And...what do you get?" he asked, cringing as he waited for the answer.

"I get everything else. Anything that comes about from the path you take on this day is mine, and that includes, upon your eventual demise, your soul."

"My eventual demise," he said, hanging on the last bit yet overlooking the words 'your soul'. "I do not want any of this *age twenty-seven* stuff," he told her, trying to sound demanding and not quite pulling it off.

She smiled wide once again. "You're *so* cute. Okay then, I'll tell you what. I will guarantee you...how about 40 years?" she offered, tapping the tip of her finger on her lips as he contemplated the offer she put before him.

Leland considered, although in his head he was weighing the offer against what he believed he would have to do to best this woman down the road. *Forty years. Would it be enough?* Leland made his decision.

"I accept your deal," he said to her firmly.

"Good," she said, and pulled from behind her back a straight razor with a shiny, pearl white handle. Leland stepped back a step.

"What is that for?" he asked nervously, holding up a hand in a defensive gesture in front of him.

"Don't be such a baby," she laughed at him. "It is merely to seal our agreement. One tiny prick of your fingertip and you write my name on this in your own blood." She handed him the rolled paper that had been in her hand. He apprehensively took it and unrolled it. There was nothing on the paper at all. It was completely blank.

"Hold out your fingertip," she said, and he did. She opened the razor and barely nicked the tip of his finger. "Now, write my name."

"Um," he started, confused that he may have missed something. "I don't know your name," he said.

"Because I haven't given it to you yet. I like to make sure you have the courage to follow through. My name is Alsindria." She spelled it for him, slowly, as he wrote the name on the paper with the blood from his fingertip. Once he was done, he reached out to hand it back to her, but she simply held up her hand. Leland noticed that part of her hand along the bottom near the palm was very dark – black almost, as if it had been badly burned.

"Take one of those matches you like to play with and strike it," she directed him, and he did as she said. "Now, light the paper."

Leland put the match to the paper and it was immediately engulfed in flames. The sudden eruption startled him and he dropped the paper, which by the time it reached the ground was nothing but a fine ash.

"There!" she exclaimed. "We are all done." She turned to walk away and started up the road.

"Wait! That's it? What do I do now?" he asked her.

Without a stop or hesitation in her stride she turned her face over her shoulder to him.

"You go out and become a rock star," she said with that bright, wicked grin. "Leave the fine details to me. Oh, and one more thing." She stopped and turned toward him one last time that night. "In forty years time, to this very day, come to see me at this crossroads one final time."

She turned, and as quickly as she had come into his life, she vanished into the darkness.

Leland Graves left the crossroads that night with a strange sense of doubt about the happenings of that evening. He didn't have doubt in himself. Quite the contrary, he had a new overwhelming sense of confidence in his ability as a musician and the path in which he wanted to take his life. He soon cast aside all thoughts of the encounter with the woman Alsindria and went about his life.

Things took off very quickly after that. A few local gigs with a few chance encounters with out of town club owners opened doors of opportunity for Leland Graves. Earnings from solo performances allowed him to be able to hire more back-up musicians, and before long, *The Leland Graves Band* was touring regionally. Leland had slowly started introducing original music into the cover sets. A fortunate encounter in a Detroit nightclub with a producer for some of the hottest rock acts to come out of the Motor City culminated in the moment that would change Leland's life forever.

Leland signed his first record deal that took him to the top of both the rock and popular charts. That first year he was nominated and won Best New Rock Act and Best New Artist, as well as Best Rock Song.

Within a few short years, Leland Graves was the hottest and most in-demand presence in the entertainment world. Magazines noted his miracle rise to fame, and he became the subject of books and documentaries within his own lifetime. He lived the life of a rock star, with the parties, the drugs and alcohol, and many, many girlfriends over that first 20 years. The time flew by, and Leland had long forgotten the night at the crossroads. Then came the Millennium New Year's Eve Rock Party of 1999. Leland played it as part of a mini-reunion tour with members from the original line up of the Leland Graves Band.

The party had been raging on through the night already when Leland and the band took the stage. He was well into the third song of a five song set when he noticed a girl in the front row with red curly hair and the smile that he realized he could never forget, wildly dancing to his song and eyeing him like so many other woman had over the past 20 years.

Leland almost forgot the lyrics to the song he was singing, but caught himself and recovered almost seamlessly, unnoticed by everyone but his own band members that had known him almost their entire professional careers.

After the set, Leland left the stage where there were several people waiting for autographs and picture opportunities. He whispered to members of his crew that he wasn't feeling well and needed to lie down for a while. The crew members waved the very disappointed concertgoers away as Leland retreated to his room. A few minutes had gone by before the noise and chaos outside of his room subsided. As he finally began to feel a sense of calm, there came a knock at the door.

"Not now!" Leland yelled out, agitated once more. The door opened, and Leland sat up and twisted toward the door, ready to verbally tear apart whoever it was that had the gall to enter his room uninvited.

He froze, and his jaw went slack. She stood there before him, looking almost exactly the same as she did that night so many years before. She hadn't aged a day, although he did notice when she closed the door behind her that the strange markings that he saw on her hand the night at the crossroads could now be prominently seen behind her left ear and down her neck.

"Well hello, Mr. Big Rock Star," Alsindria said to him. "You have done rather well for yourself."

"It's only been 20 years. What are you doing here?" he asked her, a nervous tremor in his voice.

"Relax, Leland," she said to him. "Seriously, I'm a *fan*. I love what you've done. What *we've* done," she reminded him.

"I've done it! I've done it all. Where have you even been?" he retorted. His voice had risen slightly in its volume as his anger came to the surface.

"Ah – ah – ah…" she said, and with a slight wave of her finger Leland found himself sitting back on his bed, quite involuntarily and to his sudden shock. "That is the other part of the reason that I am here. You seem to have forgotten how you got here. Not everything is magic and sorcery. Sure, it plays its parts, but you are not the only one out there to make deals with. A lot of the people in the worlds of business, entertainment, politics…they make deals too. I didn't have to do a lot of 'wand-waving', so-to-speak, to get you where you are today. I called in some favors of my own. No, Leland, you are far too valuable to me to ever allow you to fail. But you need to be reminded where you came from, and why it is that you are sitting here today."

Leland sunk down and listened to her words. He had let the fame and the fortune overtake him and his plans to 'best the Devil." He was almost regretting the deal…but only almost. He still believed in himself, and reflected on the chants of a million screaming fans over the past several years that reminded him that he had become a rock god. No one was going to get the best of him. *No one.*

Leland nodded. "I'm sorry. I know I am here because of you."

"You remember our agreement. Twenty years to go, and we meet once more at the crossroads." she reminded him.

"Yes," he replied, nodding. "Twenty years, at the crossroads."

"Good," she said, nodding, and turned towards the door. "Oh, one more thing!" She turned back around and was holding a vinyl record of Leland's first album *The Roads We Cross*. "This one is still my favorite. Can you sign it for me?" she asked, handing the record and a silver Sharpie marker to Leland. He took the two items in each hand.

"What to you want me to write?" he asked her.

"To Alsindria, my biggest fan – Leland Graves," she told him.

He wrote it and handed it back to her. "I didn't just sign another deal, did I?" he asked her.

"Nope. The one is enough. I promise you," she said, winked, and left the room. Leland dropped back onto his bed. He had a lot of thinking to do, and a lot of changes to make in his life if he was going to find a means to get out of this deal. And he couldn't wait another second. He had to start tonight.

The next twenty years moved, like for most everyone, much faster than the previous twenty. Leland came to find himself being an honorable man, and he had noted the date coming up fast over the past several months. He had actually kept his eye on it over the past twenty years, but the months leading to this moment were especially daunting to him.

His life had changed greatly since the last time he had seen Alsindria. He had been married some time ago. He had lost his wife, but not before she gave birth to a beautiful baby girl that Leland had raised on his own the past 16 of her 18 years. Alexa Jane Graves. Leland's pride and joy, and the very best part of his life.

Leland's life did indeed change in many ways, and what began as a clever gambit to best Alsindria had become a heartfelt way of life for Leland.

Tonight, all the cards would be played. He drove himself out to the old crossroads outside of the town that he had grown up in a lifetime ago. It was forty years to the very night that a young and ambitious 19 year old boy had ambled out to this spot with big dreams and plans. The moon was once again full and bright at twenty minutes to midnight, just like that night, and Leland was surprised how very little else had changed. One of the corn fields was cleared and full of only tall grass. The other three fields seemed to yield the same crops they had yielded for the past 40 years. The stump was gone, but there was a bench sitting on the corner of the roads. Leland surmised that this was probably a school bus stop in the winter months. *What a dangerous place for children to sit and wait for a bus. If people only knew what things can happen in a place like this,* he thought to himself.

Leland sat on the bench. At 59, with all of those years jumping around on stage after stage rocking the masses, his knees didn't hold up quite as well as they used to. Midnight was only minutes away. The silence of the night was broken by the sound of an engine in the distance, followed by the appearance of a single headlight coming toward him as he waited at the crossroads.

Leland narrowed his eyes and could make out a black Honda Shadow coming up upon the intersection. It slowed to a stop a few yards from Leland. The rider kicked down the kickstand and dismounted the cycle. The rider's hands reached up and pulled the helmet up and off, and a mass of thick curly hair fell from the helmet and down her shoulders. Alsindria shook her head left to right and her hair loosened and spread out around her neck and shoulders. She placed the helmet on the seat of the cycle. She was wearing skintight black leather pants and a black leather motorcycle jacket that was zipped tight up to her neck. She zipped down the jacket and removed it, placing it alongside the helmet on the seat of the Shadow. Beneath the jacket she was wearing a tight white tank-top.

"It's good to see you, Leland," she told him as she walked over toward the bench where he was waiting.

Leland once again saw that this woman had not aged a day. He was also well aware that *woman* was a term that was a far cry from the truth. Alsindria was a different creature altogether, something dark and outside the natural order of things. The blackness that he had seen on the occasions of their previous meetings had spread to the rest of her neck and her left cheek.

Leland stood up from the bench. As he rose to stand, his knees made a sound that was similar to bubble wrap being popped. The years on him were showing.

"You've looked better," Leland remarked, nodding to Alsindria's neck and face.

Alsindria grinned at his candor. "By the sound of those knees. you've had some better days yourself."

"Touché," Leland remarked back. "So, now what?"

"Now is the time we settle our debts," Alsindria told him. "You've had everything you wanted. People love you. You're music will endure in its relevance for generations to come."

Leland nodded. It was time to make his move.

"You know, I've done a lot of research over the years. I've used my resources to travel the world. I know what you are, and how your kind work. You are a demon — a real, true to life demon. The old texts — not the biblical sources, but the ones that go back much further than that — describe creatures of your nature that punish those who have gone astray. Not Hell as we know it, but something else. You feed on the souls sent to your world, but the ones that come willingly…well, they taste the sweetest, don't they?"

Alsindria said nothing, just narrowed her eyes at Leland as he spoke.

"I may have made a deal with you. I may have come willingly to this crossroads, and signed your name in my blood. But I am no good to you. Over the past 20 years, I have worked hard at living a good life. A pure life. I have done work for the homeless and the hungry. I have funded soup kitchens in 30 different cities around the country. I have gone on mission trips to some of the poorest nations in the world and built churches and schools. At first, it was an attempt to save my own ass, I'll admit. But this work…it changed me, more than I could have ever imagined. I am a new man. I started a foundation that reaches out to the impoverished both within the borders of this country and throughout countries around the world, finding placement and homes for children looking for a better life. I have personally mentored young men living on the streets of southern California to get them into programs to escape drugs and alcohol, and I haven't drank a drop myself in nearly 15 years. So I tell you this — no matter what the man was that came to you all those years ago and made that deal with you, I am not that man. What you have given me has allowed me to do so much good in this world."

Alsindria let her shoulders sink and a frown came to her face.

"Your soul...it really is worthless to me now, isn't it?" she said in not much more than a whisper. "The good you have wrought dampens its sustenance to me. Its sweet rush."

Alsindria turned away from Leland and began to step back toward the Shadow. For the first time in years, a rush of relief and hope filled Leland. He held back a smile, not wanting to taint the moment with a touch of arrogant pride.

Then, Alsindria stopped in her tracks.

She turned back around toward Leland. "Wait...this foundation that you started to help the impoverished. Does it happen to be called the StarRight Outreach Foundation?"

"Yes...why?" Leland asked.

"You hired a man to run the StarRight Outreach named Peter Hill?"

"Yes...he's worked with organizations like this for years," replied Leland, unsure of the direction in which she was going.

Alsindria let the grin take hold on her face. *That* grin! "Peter Hill has done what he has done for a long, long time, but it was your funding of the foundation that really gave him the means and the power to do what Peter does best – which is run the biggest human trafficking organization the world has ever seen."

"That...that's not possible," Leland muttered, feeling a heaviness begin to rise in his chest.

"It's more than possible, Leland. And it's all thanks to you. Peter brings in countless people looking for a new life every day, and many are sold into personal and sexual servitude. You did this, Leland. And those boys you mentored over the years. You remember Brian Franks? He spent a lot of time in your home several years ago. He was stealing items from your home and selling them on the street. He used that money to buy his first batch of heroin, which he in turn, over the course of several years, got hundreds of kids hooked. But you wanna hear the real kicker?"

"No…stop…please," Leland pleaded, dropping to his knees as the pain in his chest grew sharper.

"The real kicker," Alsindria went on, "is that it was Brian that got your lovely wife…what was her name…Ellen, hooked on heroin. The same heroin that killed her when your little daughter was only two years old. Alexa found her, didn't she? You did that, Leland! You made it all possible. Did you also know that one of your bandmates drugged and took advantage of young women when you were on tour year after year, one at almost every city you played at? No, of course not. Your manager would pay them off to keep them quiet. And there was always more, Leland. Even when you were unaware of it happening, it still happened, and you were so blind to it all. You have sent us *so many* souls over the years, Leland. And you've inspired generations to come. Young men and women will look to their idol, the great Leland Graves, and they will want to make their deals as well. One way or another, they will, Leland. They will."

Leland's breathing was getting heavier as he pulled himself over to the bench. He didn't have the strength to get himself up onto the bench, so he leaned himself against it and tried to calm himself, but the pain steadily grew.

Alsindria knelt on one knee beside Leland and whispered to him.

"Oh, Leland…to think such an upstanding and charitable man like yourself would try to back out on an honest deal that you made so many years ago. If you think you know so much about me, then you should have known better than to try and outsmart me. You're soul is nearly useless to me. A light snack, and nothing more. Want me to let you in on a little secret?"

Leland said nothing, trying hard to lift his head to look Alsindria in the eye. Alsindria helped him, gently cupping his chin and raising his eyes to hers.

"*I don't want your soul.* It's yours to keep."

"Wh…what? Why would you…?" he started ask, but was then distracted by distant headlights far down the road. Alsindria stood upright and faced the oncoming vehicle.

"Ah, perfect timing!" she said aloud, a hint of excitement in her tone.

"Who is that?" asked Leland, struggling to speak.

"All of that research you did, and you missed some of the most important parts. You've seen it for years. You've noticed what is happening to my skin, except, it's not skin deep. It's far deeper. This is not my natural form, but I can't go around looking like I actually look. People would freak out! So, we use human bodies, but they are very difficult to maintain. Over time, they wither and degrade, even beyond the power that we have to hold them together. This one lasted over one-hundred years, and she had a weak soul at best. Bit of a whore, actually, but she made good on her deal…as did I."

"B…but…you said you didn't want my soul," Leland told her, bewildered.

"Why would I want your soul? A truly pure soul would carry me over a *thousand* years. And you don't come across one of those every day. Especially one I can get my claws into. It takes planning and strategy," Alsindria said to him.

The vehicle, a rented Jeep Wrangler, pulled up and stopped alongside the Honda Shadow. The door opened, but the occupant was obscured by the headlights of the Jeep as the driver got out of the vehicle. The driver stepped forward into the view of Leland and Alsindria.

"Daddy!" yelled Alexa Graves as she went running toward her stricken father beside the bench at the crossroads.

"Alexa...baby...what are you doing here? You have to go," he muttered with what remaining strength he had left, his eyes shifting from Alexa to Alsindria. "You have to go, Alexa, now!"

"No...no Daddy, you're not well. I need to get you to a doctor right now." Alexa looked to Alsindria.

"Can you help me?" she asked Alsindria as she tried to lift her father alone. She was smaller in stature than Alsindria, with blonde hair that came to just above her shoulders.

"Such a sweet, sweet girl. Such a *pure* soul," Alsindria said with her wicked grin.

Leland shot a defiant glare at Alsindria. There was suddenly a new found strength in him.

"No! No, you cannot have her!" he shouted at Alsindria with his limited strength. "Alexa, why are you here? How...?"

"You sent me the plane ticket, Daddy. You texted me the GPS to this spot when I landed. You said this was where you'd be," she answered, confused. "Didn't you?"

Alsindria pulled Leland's phone from her own pocket and handed it to Leland. He took it and stared at it, and set it down on the gravel road. He looked back at Alsindria.

"That's what this was all about. From the very beginning. You never wanted my soul, did you?" he said, feeling overwhelmed with defeat.

Alsindria nodded her head. "Finally. You're catching up." She took a few steps back and stretched her arms out to her sides. Suddenly, Alsindria was completely engulfed in flames. She didn't make a sound. Alexa screamed a terrible scream as she watched the woman burn hot and fast, reduced to nothing more than a pile of ash in front of her and her father. Leland watched, and while he felt a subtle satisfaction in watching Alsindria's body burn, dread overtook him as he watched Alexa's demeanor change in the way that she stood watching the ashes on the ground.

Alexa turned toward Leland. She knelt down and looked him in the eye. Leland could see the tiny red pinpoints in his daughter's eyes.

"Baby...?" he whispered. She grinned at him again, that all too familiar and terrible grin.

Leland broke down into tears as the pain finally came into its full potency like a fist squeezing his heart. His eyes glazed over as the life within him slipped away.

"Poor Leland. You know what's really sad? You didn't even need me. You could have done it on your own. You were that good. At least you still have your soul. Everything else is mine."

Alsindria, in the body of Alexa Graves, put on the black leather motorcycle jacket, noting it was now a size or two larger than it needed to be. She strapped the helmet on her head, kick-started the Honda Shadow and turned the throttle, spraying up a high tail of rocks and dirt, leaving the crossroads in the distance behind her as she rode the steel horse out into the endless night.

Once Upon a Wicked Eve

Rick Jurewicz

I am a Butterfly

I am a butterfly. I fly, and I am much smarter than people think I am. I am warm in the light of the summer sun, and I travel from branch to branch, leaf to leaf, and I see the world in ways that no one else sees. I am free, and I have soft, scaly wings of the most gorgeous iridescent hues of blue and green.

I am aware of the world in ways that one cannot possibly imagine a creature of my kind would be aware of. I see the same things that man sees, the horrors and the beauty, and while fully aware, I let little of it bother me. I watch them from the air above their heads, and I watch from the window ledges of the places they call their homes. They claim these dwellings as their own, but they are also the homes of my kind, fluttering and flying about, as well as a host of other crawling insects of all different species and kinds that live amongst them.

We feed on their scraps. We feed on the sweet nectars of the plants they keep as mere decoration. Some of us even feed on their blood.

I fly, and I am free. I care little for the lives they lead, and the lives they destroy. I am a part of the world and I am free. I go where I want, in the air and through the trees and the fields and frolic across the grassy hills.

And then, hands reach out for me. A voice whispers such sweet, soft words. The hands surround me, embrace me. Their warmth is soothing and I know that I am safe within them. They love me. They tell me they love me, and I am safe and warm and loved.

But the warm hands, they slip me into a glass cage. A jar, with a shiny silver lid, turned tight overtop of me. My wings flutter, and I can see my freedom, but I cannot go anywhere. And into darkness I am sent.

The next light I see is not of the sun. It is dim and pale, with a buzz that shakes my very being. All else around me is cold and grey. I am within the walls of a dwelling of sorts.

The hands that once gave me warmth and comfort, while warm still by touch, have a new coldness in them. There is pain; my left wing is pinned to wood, and then, the same thing happens to the right. A needle pierces my center, and all is dark again.

I awaken later, yet I do not know how much time has gone by. My wings are gone now. I can feel pain. I am weak and I can no longer fly. Something else keeps me here now in this chair. My eyes are closed, and I am weak. My breath is labored.

But I am okay. I am a butterfly.

I am a butterfly.

"I am a butterfly…," I whisper with my eyes still closed tight.

From my eyes trickle a mixing of blood and tears.

"What was that, my dear?" a soft, terrible voice whispers back from across the room.

"I'm...I'm...," I try once more, but the words will not come.

My eyes open, and I fully realize the pain. The drug running through my veins numbs my senses, but does little for the pain itself. I try to scream, try to even cry, but all there is left is senseless, foggy delirium. My head slumps to the side, and I try with all of the strength I can muster to see what it is that catches my eye on the steel table to my left. I squint through the tears and the blood obscuring my vision, and then I recognize what it is.

My wing...my left arm, apart from me, on the cold steel. I began to shake as I find the strength to look to the right, and there, on an identical surface is my right arm. Nothing neat or precise, just laying there cold and white, surrounded in red.

I let my head go limp. My chin drops to my chest. My clothing is soaked in sweat and blood, some dry, and some fresh and wet. I hear the icy echo of footsteps now in the cool cinderblock room, and I raise my eyes as best as I can. I can see the brown leather shoes on the floor in front of me. I watch a hand come up slowly to my face, and it gently cups my chin, raising my eyes slowly to his.

He smiles, his warm smile, the smile that wooed me and brought me into those warm hands to begin with. Love is blind. Hands are warm. And hearts...sometimes hearts can be black, bloodless, and colder than ice. Yet still, a warm smile. But it's not for me. It is for him, and only him, and for now...for this moment.

"Hello, love," he says to me in a whisper of warm breath that is often felt in the moment of the sweetest kiss. The hand that does not cradle my chin grasps something shiny, long and sharp. The pale light of the room catches its razor edge at just the right angle, and it flashes in my eyes. I start to breathe faster, my weakened heart races as he raises the blade near the left side of my neck.

 I am a butterfly, I think to myself.

 I am a butterfly. I am free…

 I am a butterf…

Once Upon a Wicked Eve

Rick Jurewicz

Acknowledgements

There have been many people along the way over the last few years since this writing adventure had begun that I owe a great deal of thanks to.

First and foremost, the support and love of my family, Nikki and Dylan, and of course the ever exuberant encouragement of Kaitlyn. For the enthusiasm, love and support of my Dad, my deepest love and thanks, and as always and forever I thank my Mom, wherever else she may be she is always in my heart. There are a great many other friends and family members that have been so incredibly encouraging and supportive along the way, and if I were to try and list them all here now, I know there is someone that I would inadvertently leave out, so I will just say THANK YOU from the bottom of my heart!

A special note of thanks goes out to my cousin/sister Dolores Guy and her family for helping me to get the rocket off of the ground with my first novel *In the Shadows of Fate*. None of this may have happened in this way without you.

Personally and professionally, the help and encouragement that I have received from my cousin John Dropchuk has been an incredible and enlightening experience. The assistance that he has provided from a marketing standpoint using his design talent and skills to create a fantastic website for my writing, and the utilization of his artistic eye to produce promotional materials, and most recently, the exhaustive time spent in designing the cover to this very book you are reading now, has been invaluable. His work has been a great asset and has relieved the burden of having to produce many of these items myself, which has allowed me the freedom to concentrate on the writing. I cannot thank him enough for all he has done to help realize not only my dream personally, but a shared dream we once had as kids to work together to bring our dreams and fantasies to reality for others to enjoy.

A heartfelt thank you to Madison Smith for contributing her time and talent to help create a little visual accompaniment to my stories with the illustrations she helped to create for the tales in this book.

In getting things off the ground, my long time employer, Ken's Village Market - and the Swadling family who owns Ken's - have been so incredibly supportive in my writing adventure, and have gone above and beyond to help me promote my books, going as far as having an exclusive stand-out display of my books since the very beginning of their printed life, as well as being the very first place to allow me to sell my books to the public. For all of this, I offer my deepest gratitude.

And to Alex Ness, who I met at McLean and Eakin Booksellers in Petoskey, Michigan, back when I was only halfway through writing *In the Shadows of Fate* – thank you for always being both entertaining and encouraging. It has been a truly rewarding experience to make some fantastic new friends along the way. I greatly look forward to the adventures the future will bring!

About the Author

RICK JUREWICZ is an avid lover of fantasy, sci-fi, horror and dark drama, and has been writing short stories and poetry most of his adult life, some of which has been featured in print publications and online. ***Once Upon a Wicked Eve – Dark Tales and Dreadful Wonders,*** is Rick's second book publication.

His first full length novel, a dark supernatural drama, ***In the Shadows of Fate,*** was published in 2017. A sequel novel is currently in the works.

Rick and his family are lifelong residents of Northern Michigan.

Rick Jurewicz

Made in the USA
Middletown, DE
16 June 2024